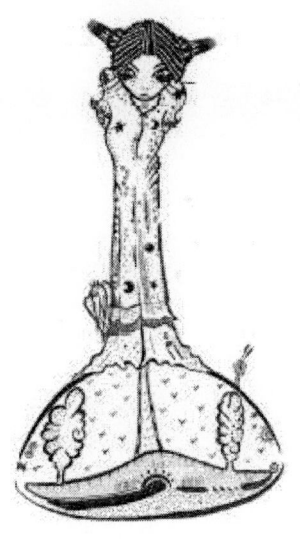

Kate's Cellar.

Written by Lawrence .R. Hall 2010.
Drawings and photography by Lawrence .R. Hall copyright 2010.

First published by Lawrence .R. Hall in 2010
London

Copyright © 2010 Lawrence .R. Hall

ISBN number 0956588302.

Printed by PMM Group (UK) Ltd

: With thanks to Amelia Hall :
And Steven Sadgrove-Hall

First edition.   The beauty Halo, Ad astra.

Kate's Cellar ©

By Lawrence. R . Hall

prologue

Kate's Cellar; is a small ancient parcel of green forest land that

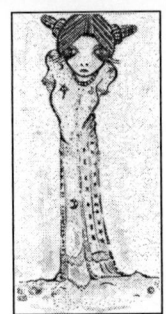

sits 300 feet below Loughton and the great Ambresbury hill, which in turn sits in a secluded steep sided mint green valley that's broken by the winding Loughton brook, within Epping Forest, Essex. For hundreds of long stringy years, stories, myths and questions have been asked by locals, why is this beautiful secluded piece of forest called, Kate's Cellar? as you will find no solid signs, except those on ancient and modern maps that gives any clue to her existence at all, but she did exist even her beguiling image survives to this very day and there were a few short articles printed in the past of whom people said she was a hermit, loner, others said beautiful beguiling tiny WITCH!

As this is what she truly was an English Gothic Witch, five foot tall, with a jet black flowing dress that twinkled with shiny exploding twinkling stars! And mystical blue swirls running up and down her thin pale arms, A true beauty of her time as she roamed the 14 th century green forest, then called the Waltham, after Waltham Abbey, which lies close by, and event to this very day you can still find some pointers to her fragile existence. (all this is open to rigorous debate of course)

So I will start as you do, at Earls path, that "locals" once called pole lane, that runs up the great Ambresbury Hill, in direct alignment to the Great North star that sits above the Hill, hence one of Kate's names pole star Kate! It is this little winding path that leads you to Kate's Cellar and Kate's small lost mellow bridge, that flows over the winding Loughton brook. Lots of other strange names survive from the tail, like Hang boys slade, (Kate's huge wolf dog) this sits behind the great hill, black weirs pond, behind to the right of the hill, Debden's slade, the lost pond, little and big monks forest, Alderton Hall in private hands and should be respected as so, these are just some.

Then there's Hope Cove on the rocky red Devon coast, the Thunderstone near Burgh island next to hope cove, the ancient Hope and Anchor inn, Greystone a huge ancient Neolithic stone that jets out from bolts tail cliff, over the deep blue English channel, St Nicolas church that used to sit so very quietly off the main road in Loughton (only 18 th century drawing still exist, which strangely shows huge black crows circling above?) and of course Kate's Cellar a parcel of green forest land below the great hill, named after Kate and till now has been lost in pure white time. Most of these names go back to the year 1313, but it is hard to tell in the modern sticky clean world what is completely true and not bent sideways? As time fades facts bleachy blue white, so you must take this story as a simple folk law tail, that probably happened somewhere back in hidden time itself, you may find contradictions, you may find faults, you may even fine bad grammar! As a English speller I'm certainly not, wordsmith I like to wish. Mostly just a writer of plain English words, so please take my round rolling words and see how far you go.

Then finally to tiny gorgeous Kate herself, and "her" story, lost for hundreds of cold bleak years, brought back from dusty old archives and long lost poems this beautiful medieval tail of a true English polestar Witch, some said futuristic star girl, I hope you enjoy reading it as much as I enjoyed finding and writing it back in her rightful place, forgive me Kate if I've got anything wrong as 700 years is a very very long time, as this is no book, this is History dancing back to it's own warm destiny.... hello.

{;DEFINITION ANCIENT GREEK:}

"HE KATE"

THE BEAUTIFUL GODDESS OF ANCIENT MAGIC,
WITCHCRAFT, THE NIGHT, MOON, STARS,
STRADDLES CONVENTION, HER WEAPON IS HER
BEGUILING BEAUTY.
AND HER SWEET SWEET HEART.

. . . .

KATE'S CELLAR

CROWS CROW, OWLS HOOT, DOGS HAIL!

It is the good sweet mellow year of **1313**. Old England lives, as a black heavy storm rolls deep and somewhat dark across the ancient high misty Ambresbury, sitting silently and secluded in the dense forest of the Waltham. A figure small in frame and form stands defiantly, reaching up to the Great North Star that sits so perfectly smooth above the beautiful tree-hidden hill.

She is skin naked to the waist, yet her small mint frame is clothed with brilliant swirling spiritual zigzag colours of blues and yellows, which sit happily alongside her jet-black hair and huge eyelashes that protrude from her black painted eyelids.

KATE is her name, Her flavour is mystical, beguiling, and somewhat awkwardly beautiful, as she weaves her chiselled ivory twee body against the growing black mass that swirls warmly around her then from above

As she dances, thousands upon thousands of tiny glittering golden leaves swirl around, around, and upside down in pure medieval motion. All are as one, with huge black red eyed crows, circling above the different colours that rise from the energy below. They screech terrible sounds that chill the swirling air. Kate speaks out openly to the massive storm that wraps her to the very inner core as she dances around and around, spinning like a wild fruitful child, energy is everywhere!

KATE

Hello, hello hello! Are you there? *(Echos across the valley.)*

Lightening strikes
sideways, like English sword on skin, crows swoop low and fast with piercing dreadful dark screams of words and danger that spin and turn wildly, as the storm rips at the hill spinning faster and faster. Then (thunder) snaps! quite lives briefly, momentarily, and then, in the very centre of the misty great hill that sits overlooking the ancient forest is Kate. She laughs a cheeky little childish laugh. Yet this small ivory white awkward being is no child. Some said sixteen but others knew she was nearer twenty-four or even twenty-five. And as this little creature of nature laughed,

the rain came back, slowly at first. Then as her laughter grew so did the rain and night joined in too.

For three whole fluid days the rain does not stop. Rancid clingy mud becomes its closest friend and most of the forest becomes impassable. Then the next day under the roots of a heavy old oak that sits on the stream floor, Kate sits tucked up in a warm grey star covered blanket that covers her head and body in one, she peeks out like the little girl she's not as silver
rain still falls heavily, smashing into the Loughton Brook that lies beneath the heavy old twisted root she sits on. Words come free, unbent and warm, uncontrolled and running like a child without measure as she then beams down at the different patterns of swirls that flow freely beneath her. She openly whispers as the rain folds up into pools then drops down into the brook. watching like a child again with energy and excitement, yet with no movement but her small almond eyes. They dart back and forth, back and forth, as she peers into the crystal blue stream that flows like music beneath her.

KATE   *(whispers in a soft velvet voice)*

Polestar, mother of Ambresbury.
Sister to He Kate tell me, "whisper" sweetly. (looks left then right)
What is this energy that comes, this vanity of fate that smiles?
As my little heart, beats me up and down up and down.
I will surly die from the inside out, does he come?

O ,,,o ?

He comes, pole star, he comes!!!

Kate jumps up and rushes away into the dense wet clingy forest, followed by two huge black spiky hedgehog crows, ducking and diving with seemingly laughing evil voices.

Four square dark, wet, misty days pass. From out of nowhere, a stranger, glowing with vibrant yet tired white energy, enters the great ancient green forest of the Waltham. He rides a huge black pumping stallion with nostrils flared blood red at the sides and a layer of black rancid mud that cakes his very being.

A knight, SIR EDWARD be, in full smashed dented amour bounds his way heavily through, as the heat rises from the muddied pair. He is battle worn yet chiselled and strong. They screech to a halt, Sir Edward lifts his rusted smashed helmet, that has clearly seen too much action, it opens with a metal-to-metal grating sound and the horse spins violently around in a knowing circle. Little can be seen in the heavy downpour, and he pulls out the battered and well-used sword, English, but still he sees nothing, and then screams deep and hard!

    SIR EDWARD

    Come on !!!!!

Black, huge beady-eyed crows spring slowly into life.

Kate looks up. Her eyes are like round black saucepans as she sniffs gently into the nothingness that surrounds her very warm tender being.

    KATE

    It's him   (she whispers then gulps)

Crows screech out like stabbed men in crying red battle.

Within seconds, she is standing "firmly" head down on the tiny bridge that
sits so peacefully at the bottom of the great hill. Sir Edward glimpses through his
rusted, smashed helmet at the small-framed object that stands ahead of him. He
moves on in, yet the great black strong vibrant pumping horse doesn't like it.
Nervously he spins sweats and weaves, as does much in this part of the forest.

He pulls up, Kate doesn't move, yet her eyes fix him like solid glue set for a thousand
long years. Rain rolls down the ivory-white chiselled face, and for a short time,
silence does rule king, as nothing is said in solid words, yet plenty is said in pure
stance and time. Small pins of the rain on the worn armour turn to a more thumpish
noise, which breaks the deafening silence that covers like a heavy white cotton
blanket. Water is everywhere as Sir Edward's warm breath hits the damp cold forest
air, it swirls like mystical soup as he tries to focus; squinting, he knows what he sees.

As this hardened knight of steel and war is already simply spellbound by this
beguiling spiritual wet beauty that stands before him. Her shoulders are back and her
head is down yet the eyes, they are fixed; fixed taking in every mere secondary
moment of this brief encounter. Then from the hill comes a deafening nasty boom as
something big and dark bounds on in. Sir Edward again spins his horse, as a huge
ugly spiky wolf dog arrives, yet he doesn't attack, just simply slips on down and lies
at the side of the muddied stream. Heat from the beast and horse mixes with the cold
rainy air and the small ivory-framed Kate awkwardly smiles as rain rolls down her
warm round cheeks that sit so peaceful on her pale structured face.

SIR EDWARD {knight}

Hello,,,

KATE   (WHISPERS LIKE A CHILD)

hello

Blue Lightening bolts across their heads, as Edward nearly falls off the spinning beast, as mud flies everywhere!

Kate stamps her tiny naked feet into this thick sticky brown mud, steps back and looks down. Sir Edward watches, spellbound in the storm. Kate's head slowly lifts at an sweet fragile twee angle, and then it drops back to the pattern in the mud her feet have just left. Again, her head lifts slightly, as her beguiling eyes" fix" Sir Edward. Rain is now so bad the stream starts pushing crystal cold bubbling water over the tiny bridge, and both are soaked to the very raw skin as the water sweeps the bottom of Kate's dress along like a fish wagging its tail back and forth, back and forth like a clock yet to be invented.

knight

who are you?

Kate's head rolls to the side,water drops off the ends of her hugh long black eye lashes as she blinks to him.

KATE {whispers}

I am Kate, "he Kate" lily of the Ambresbury? (points up the steep forest hill)

knight

Kate of the Ambresbury, I see may I pass, before we drowned!

Kate

We are drenched in silent apple??
   You won't drowned, you are blanket warm welcome. (she smiles)
   You are…….heaven sent crisp! (Kate's lashes flicker to him again)
    it is already written. (smiles) In stars be?

Sir Edward looks puzzled as Kate moves forward, with strange and awkward slow
movements. Stopping at his side she looks up, he looks down. Thunder smashes
again across the valley; she then reaches slowly up as more rain rolls down her young
stunning face. She feels at the heavy amour, running on to the horses heated side and
then her small fingers reaches the heavy point of the sharp sword, pricking her pale
ivory skin, blood flows rosy red into the crystal flowing stream to her side, then she
pops the digit into her small perfect round mouth, Kate is all eyes on Edward then
she
looks over the edge of the tiny bridge into the bubbling crystal water.

          KATE (whispers and pulls sad face)

I see….Danger ! It swims freely "Ween do you see it? Do you see the colour!
It is life,,, I is d,,,???

Her mouth opens and
On saying this she jerks back, and slips down the small mudded bank, then as quickly
as she falls she picks herself up, brushes more mud seemingly over herself, chucks
over a tiny killer smile that makes the knight blink with blinkered eye.
Sir Edward, stunned, momentarily looks up at the thousands of tiny golden leaves

now falling slowly around them, The horse rears. Then she's gone; completely vanishing into a nothingness that leaves the knight confused and somewhat mystified. He looks left then right as the ears on the stallion stand pointing upwards, Twenty heavy black spiky crows swirl and duck high around the tiny bridge in the downpour. And a lone wolf dog wails out "hollow" in the distance, sending a boom across the drenched tree-lined valley.

SIR EDWARD

Come on !

As he charges up the tiny wandering path that looks more like a stream itself, as the huge oak trees that line both sides bend and creak over him. Yet he pushes on, sending waves of water into the freezing damp forest verge and through into the low-lying black silky clouds that carpet the very misty hills, until he reaches his new location and his new warm welcoming home of colour and oak.

(ALDERTON HALL IN 18 TH CENTAURY)

A very cream smudge later, deep within the soaked forest, Kate sits tucked up, ankles held rocking slowly beneath her beautiful star studded hooded cloak that simply drowns her hole being, only her hugh black lashes protrude into real life and rain, her mind is working in shadows dancing with clouds, skipping with angels as she collides with neutron stars.

She is living "talking " in her own warm welcome, deep within the recesses of inner self.

Dreams within a dream.

It seems I'm living, if that's what this is inside my own medieval tumble down mind, but that's fine as my tumble down smiles it's happy, only sees the good in things, the warm.
So I believe
Believe in stars
Believe in brilliant medieval spinning stars, that spin my mind, stars that shine, smile, pulse, Burn!....Diamonte singing stars!

Stars that are brighter, deeper then any other seen before?
I want to cast a wish whilst dangling over the very edge of such a star.

Send out a message in time.
Want to watch as it cuts through the dark sticky, a message of hope love warmth.
I....I want to scream from my very very tender lungs.

Hellooooooooo!!

It's me
Kate!

That would be fair out happy, it would make me feel good and it's how they say?
All good things comes to those who wait! So I wait

wait

wait

and wait !!

But nothing comes back.
I'm a Hollow back girl ! With no knickers? (my tiny pale face drops in surprise, my
little eyes widen.)

I'm Empty within (isolated)
Out in the cold   (solitude)....I rain from the inside?

So I knock at the door of life, it's yellow that stands out from the dark and yes I
knock, only gently mind.....still clean nothing, it even has form shape!

I told you hollow back! I look up at the windows of life.

She's out, nobody's home! No lights to welcome, nor have a seat or give me a warm
cup of something and a cream bun! Not even a smile, so I stand on the cold doorstep
of life, watching, well nothing really, maybe that is me I'm etched. A etched nothing!

Silence sees his opportunity and stands with me, leans against the wall with booth
hands buried deep within his warm cotton pockets, he looks, judges as he stands in
his very best suited silence.

I whisper to myself, keep the secret within; I don't like him, but I keep on side, never
know when you might need him, I nod again, chuck out a roller of a smile and then
suddenly I feel brave, I'm not sure why, so I will knock again.

Show her who I am!!

Yet I'm a little worried as I might wake someone! Disturb the peace and and maybe just maybe there are kids asleep up stairs, all toasty warm and cozy and it's taken hours on hours to get the little darlings off and I will take them from heaven, take them from candy sleep, all ten eyes will cry me out pointing screaming down at me that's the one she woke use after all or hard work! Look that's her!!!

So you can see I'm in a dilemma, with a large D!
So I
Stand nervous unsure or be grown…knock so I do!
Confidence is a good thing see, In moderation I mean, I say this out loud, it makes me taller, stronger (I straighten my back, I'm not hollow back after all !) there told you, pretence is also a beautiful animal, it hides all the awkwardness in life, a wall to hide behind, so I grin back a warm welcoming smile, I get prepared. A smile that's round, not sharp edges and says hello in a cheery kind of way, like a child, yes that's it and you should always be kind to children right!

But nothing comes….yet I'm still polite!
Politeness is a beautiful key it will open most things that are worth opening and so.. wait? What's…listen something comes, I hear footsteps on wood, movement of the moving kind.

Coming towards me. I step back in anticipation.
Hold my feet together as good girls always do, well most of the time and yes their together 1.. 2 both tied up so they won't run away!

As fear looks on from the corner (I don't like corners) he points I'm nervous he laughs, so I fix my face solid turn my smile up so it says hello, it's just me o o o I hear the bolt, it's heavy rusty, it slides iron.

I think I'm on ! So I hold my breath, look up sweetly, it opens, all my fresh air gets sucked in as two brown eyes look me up and down.
This does not take long, I'm only little and my eyes do the thing, the thing being get me out of here Kate there's two of us, only one of you, so we decide please please! But my feet has orders, don't surrender to the fear, but they didn't sign up for this and now they jigger from side to side in sheer panic, they want out, it's them who has to do the talking and they do, but with my mouth.

IS IT YOU   (I ask in weaken voice)

But still nothing comes down, it's all one way today, all take and no give that's another thing girls don't like and and this waiting business is not what it's made out to be so I go again.
Helloooo it's me Kate!

I gesture in a silly girlie way, pull funny face, chuck up another smile but again its not caught and I fall to the floor with a hollow thump, I try speaking but find my head sinking, becoming heavy like lead, my eyes try to hold on, stay afloat, but lead sinks like, well lead! So I try to anchor down and that's where I'm heading, down, down drowning on the door step of life, So I give it one last go. As a girls got to try, right!

F F   FOR LOVE I MEAN!
IM LOOKING FOR LOVE IS IT HERE?

Silence steps in but I simply look around him, pretend he's not there.

I'm all eyes and very very pleased I got them words out, in the right order, ok I stumbled a little at first but once I got going it did the job! Hit the mark!

Communication is a beautiful thing, it will go far, it has a future, your see!

Hello!
Bang! Echoes through my head, how polite, dust falls the oak is closed, the passage blocked, my tiny white feet vibrate at the commotion that runs up my white sticks!

I blink the dust away, cough it back for another day!

.19.

Then to my complete surprise a small up to now unnoticed hatch slides open, it lives in the very centre of the slamming door, like a mouth on a face and it's sufficient for words to pass, eyes to see, but nothing more, nothing nasty square.

So I take what I'm given, then words do escape' roll right to me

WHO'S ASKING ?

It's Kate with a K.

I say it clearly don't want any confusion as I've come this far.

And what's your age Kate?

I look down at my feet, measure myself up.

I'm 12 years old?

12 ! comes back with confidence.

You look 10, why does a 12 look for love?

It's everyone's right to look
It's what you do, It's what I need
I'm hungry for it
I could wear it well

It could keep me warm in winter, be my friend, I could carry it always right here in my white cotton soaks, safe secure.

I see, so you think knocking at my door and asking for love is a good thing?

Well no not when you say it like that, it sounds wrong, but I mean it's what girls do
They search undercover, all eyes on alert, for prey they knock on doors, kiss many
frogs, before the prince!

I see but you cannot look for love, it has to find you, usually in the most unexpecting
ways, it will come out of the blue, if love as you call her does think something's right
then be sure the door will open, she'll charge directly at you so so fast in fact your
panic and in confusion turn and maybe even run in the very opposite direction. Then
when she finally catches you, taps you on the shoulder she say Hello found you,
doesn't mater where you are, its magic see! Dangerous magic that might hurt,
confuse, even destroy you, once meet its never forgotten, it can scratch the inside of
your eyes so everything looks different, everything will change, it will make you say
and do things you never dreamt of doing.

You will own your very own white asylum? You will be cuckoo crazy!!

Have I frightened you, do your knees knock only being 12?

No, but I'm not really 12 this is just in my head as I sit out of the rain and sometimes
I get muddled and I'm a little awkward, I'm really 26, yes I know I look younger but
that's what I am.
Sorry for the little white lie.

Well 12' 26' 99' it doesn't really matter I will let you into a little secret nobody really
gets pass 12, he's a hardy fellow and it's where most of us really are underneath.
The inner us, it's a safe place to be anyway, love will come to you have no doubt, it
can see your warm colour, you're round soft ways your like a beacon and you light
up the world. But if I may say one last thing, don't wear your heart on your sleeve, it
will dangle in the soup of life, it will get stained, so save it for someone that makes it
skip and jump, it will happen, I have to go, good luck with it all !

Kate blinks as the hatch slides across, hold on we talked about love, yes thanks for that, b..but what about sex! (Kate small pale fingers are so tightly crossed behind her back they turn ice white!

NO THANKS comes quickly back as the hatch slam shut, Kate's eyes open like clamps into the heavy rain that soak on into the real forest that sits before her, she blinks' shakes her tiny head as she looks out from beneath the massive cotton hood, then she smiles at her self in a awkward yet warm beautiful way of acceptance. I am who I am.

Kate

O dear.......

ALDERTON HALL, LOUGHTON. (A wooden-beamed, long hall surrounded by huge oaks on the top of a smaller hill that sits opposite the great Ambresbury in the forest.)

The drenched knight arrives, sodden to the very raw pink skin, he dismounts his loyal steaming horse, metal armor clangs heat and grey welcoming smoke rolls heavy out of the huge coloured painted door, and two youngsters peek out a side window to view the new dented master on his arrival at he's new home.

SIR EDWARD

I am Edward!! New sheriff be, given by King! Works done in battle, for Lord and master!

SERVANT

A true Templar of the faith they all say sir, solid oak is you! Welcome be, welcome be! my name is Steven of the Hall, Anything we can do for you.

     Sir Edward

Can you stop this downpour! (servant shakes he's head)
This water too wet, the forest too muddy the sky too black!

(crows scream high above)

Inside the timbered hall roars a huge oak warm red fire that roars like a lion up the stone chimney. Sir Edward clumbers out of his top dented amour, as a full white sheep's hide is wrapped over his tired shoulders by a girl servant. She blinks nervously at his scars that run down his muscled arms, then looks down to the floor avoiding all eye contact,whilst arranging a hugh bunch of ruby red flowers.

(Bang! as the heavy dented silvery "English" sword slides like butter into the solid oak floor),

     SIR EDWARD

What's the story at the little bridge …! (he's eyes widen as he views the servants)

Before he has the chance to finish, the servant woman jumps in knowingly as Sir Edward's eyes scan the multi-coloured ceiling above, in the process she brakes the stem of one of the flowers and smiles whilst hiding the flower behind her small thin ribbed back.

SERVANT

In the deep hollows! That's k, k, Kate, Sir. (She comes to life, nodes with a smile and then a small daisy twitch)

SIR EDWARD

Strange little thing, fragile, yet, strong she has power, presence.

SERVANT

Some say! (gulps) Others say d d dangerous, mystical, beguiling to men. She is that, not in doubt, many men want to spike her; many men have no guts for the work! Some say she's devil's own hermit sure! Lives below the great Ambresbury, at the bridge, pole star witch them Epping's people say. No doubt strange things happen up there with that beast. *(She moves forward and whispers to him.)* Beast of Bodmin eats five men daily, came up from Devonshire moors for one look at Kate! Don't know what he does for her! (her confidence now beams a blue white energetic smile of knowing) some say she dances with shadows, naked under polestar!!

Everyone laughs, claps and wails out, Sir Edward raises a shiny small glass.

SIR EDWARD

To the great beast of Devonshire's whaaaall! what a beast! And the little gorgeous wee Kate! drinks every one! Drink and be merry! Dance!

More laughter and clapping as thunder roars deep and dark over the hall. Everyone stops nervously for a mere secondary moment as the drinks move across the huge oak table with the vibrations of the thunder then they carry on, as the distant thunder falls silent in the very dark blurry wet blue night.

A slow week passes.

FEBRUARY 13TH 1313.

DEBDEN SLADE, THREE-HUNDRED YARDS SOUTH OF AMBRESBURY
HILL.

Kate walks alone, as she mostly is, along the stream in the Debden Slade that runs
south of the great hill that sits in the middle of this great and ancient forest. Trees
surround and protect her as she gently walks, dressed as she always is in a long black,
cotton and fine silk dress that is sprinkled with a thousand small, tiny diamanté stars
that catch every piece of light that flows her way. At the bottom, black turns to a
whitish bleached flavour that slightly trails behind her. She is simply beauty itself.
Then youthfully she takes a leap of faith across the Loughton Brook nearly dropping
a wicker umbrella thing that sometimes she would carry to fend off the millions of
tiny twinkle leaves that always fall before her as she lightly walks. She whispers to
herself as she goes with rosy cheeks on pale gothic clean skin.

Kate (voice in her head)

What is this woven thing that knits me up in
Confusion, it has a taste a feel, a force.
It owns, it smiles, it looks, I can feel it like a solid force.

A thing of cream beauty but also dark twisted danger?
I can see it, and I'm on it's path, it bends, turns, I do not know where it ends, but it
will end, and that will be ME ! (stops, thinks pulls a face, then shakes her head) and
stamps in frustration as she reaches up, breaks off a brown awkward sticky twig that
sticks out from the rest and chucks it into the shallow brook (Loughton Brook). Then
she simply steps back and looks down as it twists and turns in the slow shallow flow,

before lodging against a heavy round white pebble stone that sits knowingly in the middle.

KATE

Tis stuck. look see! Written, time, place; clear for any mortal to view. Fate has pulled up, unloaded its wares, entangled, forgotten, remembered, "I am picked like a sweet surrender daisy" going round and round,(looks up) it is life! …………It is me! I'm dizzy drunk!

Kate screams out, crows scarper sharp, then she spits into the stream.

KATE

Let it begin, I have sweet round heart, I pump, I am Kate! the game is on (She gulps.)

TINY KATE'S BRIDGE, BOTTOM OF AMBRESBURY HILL (no rain this time).

Smoke rolls gently like a soft white silk blanket across the flake of the fell. Small green grass-heads just manage to pop above the grey rolling carpet. Movement comes from under a huge, black, old oak whose arms have snapped off long ago.

The movement is Kate' sitting as the smoke seemingly flows freely around her very being as if it knows something mere mortals don't. She is as a child lost deep within her own very white private thoughts, as she weaves at something you simply can't see. Then she stops all movement, like a deer her head turns, she knows something approaches and she knows who it is.

KATE (whispers with a girlie smile)

I hear a dragon creeping. Stepping softly, gently. A warm dragon that lives in camouflage, stepping to deceive or to, "surprise ? "
He approaches, he's strong and a little wise, as he carries it with slight age, not much, but enough to hold on to. (smiles)

So I will talk in silence. (nods)
Think in words.

keep close as safety's in numbers and I am one, the one before he came and he does come, ……………………..LOOK! (points)

Edward steps out of the beautiful cream swirling mist that sits perched on top of the hundreds of ruby red poppies that line the green forest floor, Kate speaks at first with her huge eyes that flutter directly his way. Edward is nearly blinded as he blinks back, what he sees nervously tries a smile to shield himself, then Kate speaks with rolling round words that keep on flowing to the strong knight

Kate

Hello.

Edward

hello, you are Kate ?

She smiles a simple killer smile, that kills with one strike to his pumping heart. Then her head falls down to her beautiful medieval Diamonte dress and her small feet that pop out of the bottom like white lilies on the green verge, then her head comes up as she runs her small pale hands down her lime blue painted arms.

Kate

Yes I am her, He Kate of the wise deep Waltham, lily of the Great Ambresbury polestars sister and friend to all things beautiful? (she gently says)

Edward

I am Edward, knights templar second only to Essex and King, we meet in the storm.................. by the bridge (he points over)

Kate's eyes shoot across to the bridge then back to Edward.

Kate

we did, " Kate's Bridge" (her eyes fix him)

Edward

Yes! a beautiful little bridge it is too.

He smiles as he tries to look under her pale skin, Kate slightly nods.

Kate (under whispering voice)

Edward we have not been properly introduced. Yet your confidence rolls strong Your..... Words are round, somewhat smooth, they flow like the stream, with energy and life. Maybe I will drowned in the turbulence?

Kate momentarily shakes her small head in confusion, just like she's trying to shake something out, then she stops, looks direct to him, "fixed" on his next set of words.

Edward (thinks)

"you" will not drowned.
I am honorable, a true English Knight (he smiles)
I mean you no harm. As you know I
am kings man sent by vellum of right!
and if I may be so very, very bold to say. God forgive my brashness!

but my head is telling me we've already meet
and I don't mean at the bridge
there said! Out in the open! Honesty is a good fellow!

Kate just looks on, no movement only eyes piercing all so very, very deeply at him.

Edward

I am sounding foolish, but I already trust you, this is awkward as I spill my words but I have courage and will carry on. I feel a "force", a thing I can not explain! It weaves like a snake and
if truth be told I have been strange for weeks.

Maybe it's the weather ? And too many words!

Kate's head dips as she circles him slowly.

Kate

Words can be awkward, then ! Then there's the spaces in-between, and I don't want
to go there! (pulls a upside down smile)

your answer Edward, I believe your words have true meaning.
And yes we have just meet but

You came before you arrived see! Stars!   (points upwards) or

Maybe it was written in some far off mystical dusty grey book or simply in our heads
then
Maybe it was fate and fate is a beautiful, beautiful women, she can deceive twist and
Turn the finest minds alive or............. dead !

There you can see "me Kate of the Ambresbury"

Leaking "my" worth, you undo me sir ? Maybe its mystical magic of make believe
Magic of old pointing me out spinning it's game and we are now the prawns
On the table and the game has already begun We know each other for nothing
And yet it is pure something that sits at my table?

Kate turns sharply, runs her small pale fingers gently down he's rugged face.

Who will win!

Kate or the knight. who will stay in the game black or white! (she chucks up a weak
and somewhat crazy smile)

Confucius dance amongst the lilies Edward. (both just stare)

Silence again stands between the pair like a solid stone wall, it's a kind of silence that has weight, it gives them time and comforting space, then Edward bravely speaks out, in words you can here with solid ear.

Edward

So we agree! whether it's magic, fate, or madness or something so so Strong and different we can not even explain what it is, A force that brings me to your door and yes I knock, I'm here, confusion runs on both sides of this path. (he raises his arms)

Am I mad!

Kate

You are not mad, you are human you have a warm beating Heart (touches his chest) we both know this, we both feel this, a bridge Built in time from me to you, no one can explain? it is a strange beast that Swirls between us, entwining us together, and I answered the door ! We've said this! No distance matters, it doesn't have distance, we can not meddle in such Deep deep things, you are the knight and I am simply me, Kate of the Ambresbury Hill, all will be forgotten in time or ……not?

there a contradiction of a womanly kind !

your first lesson Edward (she smile) HA! (both smile)

Everything is written Edward, everything? A start a middle and an End.

Edwards eyes fall to the stunning beautiful lime blue swirls on gothic white skin that decorate Kate's thin arms.

thunder and blue lightening skips across the sky as it dances above the tree tops then silence once again takes hold, not for long but to them it is years This is then broken as Kate's whisper to the knight.

Kate

take care Edward, in time be, always take care?

She points to him

SIR EDWARD

And ....you! Take care!!!

Edward backs away, still fixed on what he thinks he's just seen before him. Kate's gone he shakes his head, Sir Edward looks back to the very place she was, only seconds ago - nothing, just the rising mist that swirls in circles and an ear-piercing scream from the observant owl, now sitting and watching from the tree.

Thunder groans like an old man creaking at the knee, leaves twirl down from the solid old oaks above.

SIR EDWARD

Kate! don't leave, d don't go.
Please we have hidden words to speak, secrets to keep, thing to do!

This is unfinished !!! Unwritten !!! Do not hide from me, not me!!!
what did I do!!

The wind pushes through the trees as it weaves in and out of the branches and then the valley, clearing the mist and leaves. The lone Knight spins around looking for her but nothing comes, just the whistle of the lone cold vacant hollow emptiness that echoed in his ears, yet the little pulse of energy doesn't give up as she searches high and low for her, as she is family, she is a friend.

Days later the tiny blow of snaky white energy finally connects with something it had been looking for, for some time, and now it had found it with a smile, things started to stir, energy started to snap spark, build in the dead of dead night.

THE BEWITCHING HOUR OF THE ADULT FORM.

Tick tock, there's no clock!
Tick tock, there's no clock!

The lime blue moon smiles, lightening dashes across the jet black night sky, with brilliant whites, blues and silver. thunder creeks and groans as it runs through the dense forest and over the great hill of the Ambresbury as this little puff of energy grows and spins with every second, humming music starts to fill the forest floors, lightening dances skips with a crack of the whip smashing and sparking pink blue in the darkness.

Hang boy (Kate's huge wolf dog unseen wails deep and low)

Lead heavy rain smashes through the canopy of the Waltham, thumping down on the tiny village of Loughton that sits nearby, it's reaching the witching hour of 12 midnight, the time spirits wake, weave their mischief below your warm cottoned beds, the time bad spirits do there work, the time bad spirits hide in your dark corners, awaiting for their time to come! And time does come, it's the witching hour, midnight as the beast of a storm spins round and round the Great Ambresbury Hill!

Energy is everywhere, building, stacking, snarling as it run deep through the forest, Hugh oaks bend and creek sideway, Loughton brook fills as it winds like a giant green silvery snake down the valley towards the small village of Loughton.

Thunder bruises ! Clouds spin colour, locals hide slam shout there wooden shutters, hide under there beds, as its 12 midnight !!!
Laughter weak at first spills from the caldron of the storm, then too like the puff of energy it grows into something more adult, more nasty and complicatedly womanly, it's Kate's laughter, it has shape edge, meaning, it knows what it's doing! As danger jumps up and down like an excited child, clapping screaming!

As the Golden white naked Ivory glides in.

Half skin naked, yet painted with scary beautiful yellows, blues, her ivory skin catches and keeps the light that sparks from the excited flashing lightening,
This is not the shy creature, the mystical shadow that catches from the corner of your

eye, this is blatant in your face power and sexual energy and she wears it with a beautiful grin that runs from ear to tiny ear, she is futuristic, then that small weak laughter snaps back into something so very, very sharp and dirty, so very very adult, that shooting stars bend sideways across the sky just to look, and Kate's tiny ivory body starts to convulse with tiny jerks, she smiles, laughs, rain smashes down on her tiny frame, pure adrenaline pumps up her tiny blue veins as pressure builds, spasms live, excitement rules as her white bleach eyes roll so very, very deep inside her blackened eye sockets as rain smashes her paint down into blurry colours that are frighteningly beautiful.

Sparks then jump from her tiny white finger tips, reds, blues, all the colours live, then she bends, arches her tiny ribbed painted back so she looks directly
up into the belly of the storm, rain smashes down, assaults her colour and she laughs a laugh so very disturbing, so very something only those who heard such a laugh could understand it, as it comes deep within her tiny chest and now lives amongst the very living! Thunder roars as it joins in, lightening strikes with a white pure CRASH!

Everything stops dead, rain laughter, and the storm, and maybe even time itself, but only
Briefly as
Silence again truly lives, as a warm glowing light appears, mist weaves in between
The lines of blue bells and pure white lilies, it's morning birds start to sing then a small girlish laugh peeks out, it's Kate, she giggles like a naughty child.
As Sir Edward's black stallion can be seen chewing at ripe grass, He and Kate are not in view, only one last childish laugh from her?

A new warm day is born.

Weeks pass silently, slowly like winters grass, Kate's gone, disappeared into a pure white nothingness. People in the local tavern talk aloud about her passing, or moving on. None are happy as the weather goes foul and animals sick. There's open talk on where she has gone to, and the shiny Knight walks the very paths that she belongs but to no avail. Only the white owls screams out, and the weather turns more cold and nasty sharp as sleety snow falls fast, yet it is still spring. As confusion makes merry, nobody, including the shiny dented Knight is happy.

Fighting History.

For days after the storm, Edward searched high and low through the misty cream ancient forest, clumping and squashing his way through the marshy black ice flack of the fell and on into the deep heavy green brown forest, all he found was his own pale emptiness that surrounded him like shadows, so The knight kept moving on, then quite suddenly, from nowhere? he fumbles down the steep muddy banks of the winding Loughton brook where he finds with a crunch under foot the bottom, he stands, looking up he sees the forest floor, ten feet up and over hanging green trees, white foggy mist twist and turn like a new born serpent, unnerved he pulls out his loyal English sword with a heavy swish! and makes his way up the shallow crystal stream, then he stops, looks up the bank, as strange glowing warm blurry lights and a humming come bouncing back down to him?

Edward

Who's there, Show yourself!

Edward keeps moving on up the shallow stream, holding out his loyal friend the sword named "English" as the mists rolls round and round in white clean circles.

Edward

Ha! Who's there! Show your self Coward!

From the mist comes back a nasty grating metal to metal sound, it's big, very big Edward has heard this sound many times before in battle, and knows what's coming towards him?

Edward

come on then, lets see what you've got? I'm Edward, second only to Essex and king! Show yourself!

Coward show!

He screams (yeah!) as something touches his face and he instantly strikes it in half, a flag of red and white hits the stream floor, Edward looks puzzled as another flag, worn and old flutters on the other bank, then instinctively he backs up slowly still waving English before him, as his eyes spot a glint of silver come bouncing through the white misty fog, Edward's eyes expand at what enters out to him, it is history pure and simple, worn and battered come to fight in armor and colour, no words are now said, Edward knows what stands before him and with a heavy crack history attacks him with heavy weight and a hugh clank of sparking metal, red yellow sparks fly into the cold fizzing as they hit the water madness erupts

Within seconds both are covered from head to foot in black sticky cold mud as violence dances with vigor and music humms sweetly, this is a personal fight between Edward and history, Edward slips back under the great weight, holding up his loyal friend above him for protection and history takes it's stance above, every thing suddenly stops history, jumps around, slashes at the nothingness in the stream, leaves start to tumble from above, history panics as it sometime does, turning once more to Edward lying in the mud some square and brackish old words are spilled to him, then history turns and carefully sword still weaving he re enters the heavy soapy fog. Edward's arm drops back down with a slash, as he can no longer hold up the English, above him, he feebly stands with a simple fumble and makes his way back to the great Hall.

On arrival the small girl servant looks on, then helps him in out of the dark and into the light she holds him, smiles, he's shaken as he lays inside the door.

      servant girl

Sir?
what happened to you, you're safe whatever it was,
Has gone it's

History! You'll be fine? Just fine, drink sir drink.

Thunder groans and creeks high above as Edward falls asleep with pure exhaustion.
The servant smiles awkwardly as she cleans her masters deep cuts and scares.
The night rolls in and everyone sleeps a peaceful warm night.

WEST; small hilly cove looking out over the deep blue English channel. as Kate stand on the very edge of a high

dangerous cliff, as the sound of the sea fills the first morning twilight of dark blues and pinks, she's covered in a long grey star studded cloak that covers her small ivory framed head, hang boy wails unseen as Kate's beautiful eyes open, parting her huge black eye lashes as she views the sea, far off shooting silvery stars travel at speed towards her and the tiny bay, for one glimpse of her, morning fishermen look on in wonder from their far off boats, colours mount up reds, greens, blues as the northern lights visit her too, crows, big black and spiky glide on down from above, she slightly smiles to the spectacle flourishing before her small frame then her tiny wee head comes up from within the heavy star studded cloak.

Her eyes open slowly as she silently gleams out to the mystical spectacle before her.

Kate (whispers)

Hello,

Destiny (her eyes flaunt and twinkle)

Are you there?
It is only me, Katie of the Ambresbury, over east way!
Hello oooooo (small giggle, lightly pulling out small lily flower tosses it gently over the edge as she watches it fall smaller and smaller finally landing in the heavy white swell amongst the sharp dark spiky rocks)

It seems I'm, erm lost, have you seen hope?

Stars shoot over the tiny cove with too many colours to mention, she smiles?

This way then, (she points)……. to hope? (Her eyes light up as)

She nods, turns, follows the worn path that go's up and down, up and down along the jagged dangerous cliff top.

Some say this is now called "star hole cove", and is surely as very beautiful today as it ever was then.

Wondering Star;

Morning brakes, twilight smiles, as the cloaked Kate wanders long the lonely path
That follow the cliffs edge, sometimes the very ground path itself disappears over the
edge into the nothingness, avoiding this peril she carries on thinking as always in her
own sweet mind as her legs involuntarily carry her on.

    Kate

I walk to think
Only my eyes see
Only my little white feet follow like baby white ducks on a still green round pond,
but this is no pond, this has ups downs, in's, out.

Cliffs, danger, beauty, life I smile to them all, and move along, staying in line, but not
straight, never do that? So I try and write.

Write words, inside my own head, some are lime blue against pink white, others are
upside down, event inside out, it's away of thinking, but this does not matter see?

"they are my words".......in my world.

And of course nobody sees.

"They are naked and dressed with white smiles"

That curves all the way round? anyways I'm greedy with words I like to look after them, round them up, keep them safe, as you don't want to lose any? Might be important, that little word that sits so quietly at the back, Maybe one day they will be the boy, the doer, the beauty, so I keep my eyes open stay in the game, walk with hands buried deep and my head clean up, anyways these words are special.

Yet to be said, virginal, clean cut fresh
they have not left my tiny mouth.
"
I've not born them" see!

Come the right time, right place,
I let them go
Hope they do their thing, hope they don't come out wrong!

Fall to the wrong person, who won't send it back with the post or with a thought or simple plain smile, that says no thanks you!

I hate waste!! and I hope my words are not to be wasted. So I move on, not in straight lines, never do straight always follow the curve, doesn't mater how tiny it is, as everything has a reason, anything that says it's straight is probably not. Follow the curve into a circle, like the moon, like life and death it will all bring you back to the very start.

A pattern in time
A pattern in being, lots of patterns out there.

But nobody see them, understands them, everybody follows these things daily, yet nobody talks about them, nobody sees! understands, but every living thing is a pattern and and! COLOUR!!

o

that's too too much for me to go into, o look at my dress, there's me off, so I need to go back to my round rolling words, they roll like my smile today ha! And I will push on up this little hill that's green cut and sits over looking the blue rolling sea!

O

I can....feel my tiny heart.

It pumps me
Under pressure through my tiny blue veins into my heart, head, lungs. I am alive, I see its me alive in history so up the hill I go, yet something's wrong.

It's not in place, my heart I mean?
Not in my cavity,
It's off line, off rhythm, something's upset it.

It's on the shelf, contained in a round tight lid jar?

It looks out in silence.
It tries breathing but its all maxed out, I think it's suffocating

It gasps! It does, it wants air!! Tooo much pressure all around and that lid is so so tight I bet some smug camouflaged smiler did it and simply walked away? So it sits on the dusty shelf of life,

Looking worried, concerned.
It has issues ok but courage holds it's hand (he's a kind fellow, doesn't say much but he stands his ground and looks, its scared, scared some other camouflage fool will smile and chuck out some clever words that sink so deep into you you fall into a dizzy fit, and once you start falling there's no stopping matters till you reach the floor with a sickening thud.

And the jar shatters into a million sharp nasty pieces.

So I've learnt, being grown.
When people stop, stare, look and point, a trick.

I start with a small girlie grin.
A flutter of lash
And a slight lowering of one's head, then the mouth curves only slightly this sends
out the message in polite English.

Helloo how are you, now please F... OFF this is when you duck yourself away, learn
to live another sweet day.

But sometimes even this little trick doesn't work and they move in for more.
Ganging up close in! and I'm close to the edge, don't want to be broken!

So I chuck out a true beamer, A blinder of the colourful kind and disappear under my
own transparent ivory skin, but no, no that won't work so I'm plain OFF!!!

Can't take nothing from nothing, eyes think!! And if I'm not there ? So I keep
moving
Moving safer no one can pin you down, take your ....

Kate's eyes open to reality Devon country side blue sky and warm fresh air she is
moving in thought as she travels.

TWO wondering sleepy months on, she is still walking.

I cross a field of golden syrup?

Yet this is not that, this if fine crisp golden wheat that stands to my shoulders, it sways alive!,, with hip and flow!
Gently it bends over and over till you think its going to snap, but it doesn't ? just waits patent till yes! it comes back again! A gorgeous thing to watch in silence and I simply do, Watch the very footsteps of life doing it's stuff ?

I can see it's feet!,,,,, this is o so English mustard, pure beauty, old school English! It's the real thing! With wheat cast by farmers very hand that makes our daily bread, this is marvellous, then I notice a space in the wheat further on, look a sweet isolated island? I feel I know him? emphasis with the nothing! and

It simply does nothing? And so is different?

because of this...... it stands out!

Now I'm myself standing in the nothing, as everything around me bends with life I smile with ever growing saucepan eyes, colour is all around.
Red red red of the most ruby kind,

I nearly gasp air! My tiny brain is exploding with colour! so I simply stand, take it all in underfoot I look down, Everything is mud bleached white dry.

Cracks hold up the land!!!

Heat is everywhere, I can feel it on my brow, my little pale arms are turning salmon pink, maybe yes, ruby flipping red! The same as the poppies that lives in circles that sit in front of my very eyes, A pattern has formed and it sits here hiding amongst the wheat, it is out of view, out of mind, but once in it's heavens daughter lying back soaking up the sun!! ha ! Everything sways, this is life and I must take it in so I do with a deep deep breath that fills my tiny lungs, it's invited, it is welcome! It is NATURE!, no pretence, nope, just little old nature doing it's thing.

The beauty nature of the sweet golden kind, a kind of nature that's family, then as I travel through again in the sway I see a edge the end? Everything is sharp, Everything just drops off, I look down, view the view that sits in front of my eyes then my brain ask what's up? Why we stopped? I look down for below me is a red gravel road? It kind of lives below it's own skin, underneath like, maybe it's shy?…a shy road that just wants to be left alone?
As it sleeps so I gently jump myself down, touch my feet with the round pebbles that line it's back, dust jumps back to replace myself, I look left, then right?

Left is up hill, right is down, so I go down and right, as I like to be right once in a while and it's easier on my sticks, so now I walk with a smile and no hood, exposed I smile, the sun is out, then in the near distance I see shape of mankind, a building with edge, form, a tall steeple of the very christian kind, pointing straight up to heaven! So I carry myself on till I come to the foot, a stunning stone church that sits isolated and I like that, look it's holy brought with tiny oak doors and strangely again it seems to be dug into the red soil again just like the gravel road! And and it seems to me like it's trying to hide before winter comes? Yet this is not winter this is heat, I sweat my brow, water is on my mind so I enter God's house, I'm sure he would not mind,

Dark, dust, stone I'm in, the smell is lovely the roof low, on I go before I stand at the holy wisdom, candles flicker different colours shadows grey silence lingers, I move on, find myself sipping holy water it's refreshing clean then I see the beauty, o o carved in golden colours, a virgin and child carved from solid oak, she strangely has the hip, the flow, she has it all going on, she is the holy virtue of the christian kind (my mind jumps to Edward then I'm back in control) Glampton church is written in words and before I'm not sure there I am outside looking in, looking over the hedge and I see the sea! Cliffs I move on……

Days pass

And many long, long green miles away in the deepest remote Devonshire hills that roll up and down up and down, lies a small round harbour that's surrounded by large, red cliffs. It is so so beautiful nobody ever leaves as the same person who visited in the first place. As remote is its key, at the centre is the inn - the Hope and Anchor. It sits so near the sea that when southwesterly gales visit, and they frequently do, they mass at the harbour wall, sending huge black blue waves over the top of the thatch and down the twisting chimney that sits below. And this is where Kate lies, feet up in front of a roaring red English lion fire.

She is wrapped in a grey-starred cotton-weaved cloak that's so big you do not notice the huge spiky dog – Hangboy - under it. She sits back alone, head covered, sitting as usual, against the wooden bleached bench. The locals all stay well away as they have seen the huge sleeping beast. Talking of sleeping, this is just what the locals say about the tiny village of thatch-roofed cottages that hangs off the sides of the red cliffs. Fish, beer and church are all that are known. And of course there's the New One, as she's known. Yet she seemingly doesn't venture to the stone-cold church that rings its merry tune, bing-bong, bing-bong, bing-bong.

Inside the Hope and Anchor Inn, Kate sits feet up covered in her grey star studded cloak no part of her body can be seen as her head is down and she dreams peppercorn dreams that slowly mysteriously melt in your mouth as the white winds of winter blow from the south, a storm rolls on in with heavy white lumps of water, they jump like children over the harbour non excitant wall and smash like adults against the Devon stone Inn, yet once inside the belly of two foot thick stone all is warm, all is silent and Kate dreams like a cat next to the glow of oak on wood.

DREAMS WITHIN A DREAM.

(Fireside, hooded and feet up, she dreams words in the warmth)

I like to breath like vintage?
    sometimes
    I breath well and that's important
    I don't do shallow, just deep and meaning.
    so I go
    In
    pause,
    pause!
    PAUSE!! (anchor anchor !) give the air time to enter, absorb, time to live.

Then it come out ! And I live once more.

    my ribs do all the work, as sometimes I'm lazy
    and it's not a good thing to be lazy about, also it keeps
    me being, as it's life, a friend,   a constant, a modern clock maybe?
    Something people will think a lot about in the future, as they will try
    And catch it with metal human devisees, but it want stop.
    so I keep on side, as I smile, this is always
    a reassuring thing to do, nod and smile in the English way

    and this is what I do, but without knowing or
    meaning, it just happened sometimes, involuntary

    without notice, so I look myself up and down, what
    do I see, well it's me (there's a surprise) small and pale, a girl with
    Big black lashes and paint, not much to that then, so I do what I always do
    When unsure I chuck out a quick smile and duck my head
    But wait, hold on and I look closer, look underneath don't duck as it's only
    Me so I see through the paint, take down the wall, ha hello me! Hello.

I jump back to reality. As the oak opens cold Atlantic air rushes in and pushes the warmth to one side then as quickly as I woke it's stamped out again, two local fishermen bundle in, and the warmth drowns over us all, I am sleeping heaven like a black cat on a beautiful mat and I fall back into my dream within a dream, silent wisdom sleeps with me as this warmth of fire penetrates, like no man,, well ok maybe one, ha I'm feeling like the halo virtue, "golden in silence" she surrounds me in the red warmth of winter, I wear white pearls of beauty wisdom as politeness sits on the other side of heaven I see him he smiles back as not to offend, twilight wants in on this moment of white magic, but he's hours away, so.....o have I lost you? Did you fall off, I will Endeavour to go back, follow my tiny foot steps back in time.

I'm sitting see in silent wisdom, only the crackle of the fire spills it's voice out onto the oak floor before me.
I'm not a loan,,, a friend of the very truest kind sits with me, not in form but in my mind, she is most comfy there and holy Angels flock, they drift slowly in, unnoticed as they don't shout or scream.... As they know who they are, they come from white heaven like snow drifting in on a winters night, they glide in motion,,, sideways everything is absorbed everything is white her name is sweet Ween, Ween of delicate beauty,

She has departed this life but lives in all spirit (I love her, I love you Ween?)

Kate smiles a beamy, crazy smile inside her own head, she knows her thinking is strange, awkward, and this is where she keeps her words, private, secure, and to herself.

Then she opens her beautiful black painted almond eyes,

That reveals the

Inside of the same inn of solid oak beamed door, where you find a long thin and low welcoming hall both ends stand with huge lion roaring fires that spin and turn up the Devon stone chimney, everything else is off whitish and oak brown as the closeness off the sea and air seeming weathers and bleaches any thing that stands still, lilies of the whitish purest kind line the walls and yellow straw fit's the beautiful carved oak benches, it is a warm place to anchor and simply hope! A true thing Kate has been doing for weeks.

Smash as a grey lump of water washes away the summer dirt from the Inn sea wall.

Hang boy lightly wails a very deep deep sound that travels across the floor, this puts everyone on tinder edge. Kate eyes all the room, and then from nowhere the fire is squashed back from high above as a mass of cold heavy sea water fills the chimney, sending a small wave across the same oak floor. Everyone jumps up to stay dry, as the solid oak door smashes violently, open, the water and air seemingly meet with hugs in the centre of the warm welcoming inn.

INNKEEPER (hope and anchor)

South westerly! Save the boats! and close that door!!

People scuttle, as a masked brown ship, with red dancing flags roll, very, very deep in the white froth beneath the huge red cliffs that stand like knowing giants looking out over the tiny, ancient village, the red and white of both spells DANGER in capital screaming letters!

Kate whispers knowingly under her warm breath (A bitches storm) as the oak door slams violently open against a beam. (even to this very day the same door does the very same thing in storms and refuses to stay closed for too long?)

Everyone runs out pointing at the nasty disaster that's about to happen. They do the sign of the cross as they hold up their hands to protect their faces, the inn keeper shouts out to look, "LOOK!" on the cliff! He points to a small grey-cloaked figure,

KATE! She's pointing herself, but she's pointing at the very dark rolling storm that lashes and smashes the tiny cove. Words strange in form and style are chucked out into the blackened sky as it weaves about her very being, they are square in form with sharp old meanings, and if you look carefully amongst them your see small pieces of dark intense matter?
That clings like rancid black mud?
Kate leans into the onslaught, as massive, monster seventy-foot wave smashes and crash over the jagged spiky rocks below and snow-white spray fills the air around the cloaked figure. She argues and screams, gesturing with strange jagged movements. Her cloak dances and weaves violently behind her like a living beastly animal! She shouts in some old brackish, English talk, as Hangboy wail's away happily in the distance.

        Kate

Energy of life!!!!!!!
Disk thee, come see! Outish my moon! Kate see ancient welcomes, yea! Tass friend be local as pole star solid be! Faithful honourable old ways still live. Not dead look, No! Others see her come, be I daughter see! Me litts Kate, yea, no, not be for see calm be sister or stab haven's heart. save ye to ramilles, Leave us be! Monster is, leave us be, come see! Hope, ye cove history!!!!!!!!!!!!!!and pure beauty!
See!!

THE GREYSTONE

She spits and thumps the oncoming wind as the locals hold tight against the monstrous rage that assaults their very being.

Then
Madly she smiles as her hair twists and turns behind her and she jumps down from the stone they now call the Greystone, still to be seen today as it jets out into the sea above the cliffs. The locals all watch as the massive southwesterly simply turns on itself and the monster waves settle back down. Everyone turns to the ship as it

rounds the Bolt Tail cliff. It is safe but damaged. Then at one last final throw of the dice, pure white lightening smashes down through the black onto a large stone pillar in the bay. When the air and smoke clears you can see right the way through! Locals all do the sign of the cross, as all eyes are now on Kate. She knows it's time to leave, this place they call Hope Cove. And the stone they call Thunder Stone. Kate leaves that very very day. Time passes, like melting ice on a cold kitchen floor.

Months later, spring does wake happily with blurry crusty eyes.

Sir Edward blinks this time it's his mind playing games, as he sees in his mind A picture of himself and Kate standing face to face in the church yard, they stand ten feet apart both stand on raised graves of stone, music flow out of the church, Edward chucks gently a white lily, Kate does not move and it falls down on to the grass below, Edward looks confused and tries again, and the same thing happens, but this time a preacher watches from the dark church doors, music swims around the grave yards, and then Kate's face twitches, Edward tries again chucking all so gently the white lily and kate folds over and catches with both hands, slowly she stands smiles, every one claps, and Sir Edward is back from his thinking and sitting for real in the church, he blinks at the dust as sun shine beams through the dark.

ST NICHOLAS CHURCH LOUGHTON

The church is small in frame and form and made of local white oak and brown round stone. Inside a small tower, sit two small bronze bells that mostly sit silent. But today they live and dance, ringing out with a sweet mellow yellow sound that floods the wooded valley below. Smoke "grey"can be seen drifting across the valley floor as Sir Edward sits listening to the local preacher. Behind him stand four pretty young females all dressed in different brightly coloured dresses that gently sway in the breeze, which flows with their voices, out of the dark heavy church and into the light of the morning warm sun. Cheekily, the music flows between the graves of the ancient church and runs free like children do, down the grass-kept hill to the forest verge. It is here that stands a girl; her name be Kate.

She stands leaning back against a broken old knowing oak, and she is simply dressed to kill. This time not in jet-black and silvery stars but a creamy-white silk and cotton flowered dress that seemingly must have been made by gods, as she beams youth, and wisdom dances happily around her.

Sir Edward breaks from his own mind, Standing, he walks to the west heavy oak, beamed door as his eyes follow the dancing, flowing warm music down the gently sloping hill to where they sink deep and fast into the merging image before him. He moves out of the heavenly Christian church and walks slowly across the graveyard as, seemingly, all the occupants hold their very breaths beneath him. This time they meet it is already different, warmer in colour, no sharp edges, just smooth round circles. The music slightly fades and Kate does one of her smiles that Sir Edward catches with both hands, and Edward is nearly already out.

Face to face, at the bottom of the hill.

        SIR EDWARD

    We meet again … in peace be.

KATE

We do. 'Tis written!{grins} in lime blue twinkling shiny stars,{her tiny finger points upwards} like polestar to pole, sun to cool blue moon. You are looking … fine, more healed in nature then before. Let me take your hand Edward we can walk in pure warm welcome, is this fine with you ?

SIR EDWARD

Yes, fine. Welcome back.

Kate does not answer at first then looks at his cut arm.

Kate

Have you been….. fighting?

Edward

yes.

She stops, gives him a look of slight disapproval, then forgives, "him instantly"

can't fight history Edward, (she smiles warm) it will catch you in the end?

He nods,
Kate

History and sweet religion are powerful beast Edward,
You are a christian… sent from powerful heaven (smiles)
You believe in something you simply can not see???
Yet you will fight for it
Till death if must,….that's a powerful force.
A faith, that swirls in time, kept together with words of wisdom be
Thousands of words set down on vellum, mystical in itself,(looks a him)
Anyways the Bible is the Bible and you are you! Nothing wrong in that
It's your taste your Nature,
Erm? (looks at him again) your colour is blue,(Edward looks at her with puzzled
expression they move off)
And me!…… the very same just different?
I Dance to my own religion, it twinkles?
Roll to my own words, smooth,
Live my own style, futuristic in form and my book is cosmology (points upwards)
Stars are made in heaven and this is my book, see everything is written Edward a
path to follow! It's written in the stars a map in time, you look puzzled,

What I'm saying is I don't have churches however nice or beautiful they are I have me I am my own religion!
It is me I am it, you can see it touch it I'm real! Hello.

Edward

That's beautiful, I will think on your words (nods)

Kate

Good, that's all I ask, some understanding she smiles a killer smile.

Both enter into the deep dark green forest until they reach Kate's tiny bridge below the great wise Ambresbury hill.

SIR EDWARD

Kate's bridge. Ladies first I think.

KATE

No Sir *(laughs)*. Not mine, Templar bridge be, Kings say so *(she smiles)*. In King's name be, written on pure vellum, *(whispers)* under key. Like stone, honest honourable keeper of the faith, Everyone will remember this little bridge Sir.

Hundreds of tiny leaves twinkle down around her as she crosses.

KATE

Earl's Bridge be, Earl's Path one day? ha! *(She stamps.)* Solid in time and space like black matter or white diamond.

She nods then spins on the spot, stops and chucks out another smile. Sir Edward's eyes and mind nearly explode with a million tiny stars.

SIR EDWARD

White diamond? sweet black matter! what are these stunning things, sounds like something, only you could ever say? (pulls upside down smile)

KATE

HA! a thing of beauty sir! fragile, futuristic in matter and solid in time? Don't worry, diamonds last forever, even if hidden under dark murky ground, but thank you for your sweet words, they are much cherished. Though not so true as I'm more fire or ice and I will surely fade like all things fade. It is Nature, it is I, it is the truth and nobody can hide from the truth. Not King or servant, tis will find you in the end, truth will out. Home be me sir *(she stamps twice on the bridge)*, pleasant of mind and body, it is good you are keeping well.

Sir Edward keeps watching as she seemingly glides off into her forest with the millions of falling leaves that always keep her safe.

SIR EDWARD

Can we meet again?

KATE

The Morrow sunrise, remember the hill? Do you rise early Edward ?

She points up the hill and disappears with a small girly chuckle, Edward watches spellbound in a moment of pure white time, a bundle of time he will keep forever.

Then
The sweet morrow comes with broken warm flickering sun.

Ambresbury Banks slowly comes to life as the never ending silence of the night breaks into warm pink colours that have no solid edge everything is blurred above the green forest floor as the gray creamy morning mist rolls clean and silently in.

Edward, stands alone in shadow before the sunlight breaks a very clean direct path through as it touches his face momentarily his eyes close then as quickly they open with words

EDWARD

Kate are you here? Answer me, Hellooooo

Silence answers back with great loud voice as Edward turns his head, yet more nothings then as he turns back. He slowly spots something ivory moving around him yet it doesn't walk in the heavy mist but glides silently and smoothly through the massive twisting old oaks.

KATE

Did you scream ?

SIR EDWARD

Yes! it was me. my God, you are Heaven daughter, your beauty is truly something magical, I would wait many moons for you KATE. don't forget what I say?

Kate silently nods and Sir Edward sees for the first time that underneath the mist is just ivory - no clothes. just swirls and beautiful colorful patterns, She smiles at him, mocking him in her own tasteful medieval way. Mist rises and the pair disappear beneath the blanket of swirling mass. That same day, but this time at the other end of it, the pair can be seen bathing together in the Black Weirs pond that sits silently behind the Great Ambresbury Hill, Both float facing each other under the thousand million stars that look on down with beguiling interest, each standing out, as their ivory whiteness clashes with the peaty dark water beneath.

KATE *(whispering to Sir Edward)*

Destiny dances Sir *(she touches her heart)*, wags its long firm tail. I skip in twilight, like a puppy be, as fear he hides in silence and very mood. Happiness wakes too, after many moons, as this blanket of pure white magic and hope covers me so, from head to foot be, glowing warmth inside. Yet it whispers too in sweet knowing ancient voice, gently sweetly danger wakes, lurks, without a care, he walks as sure as polestar to moon. demonology dances freely around the giant toothy pike? I am only little me, a silvery minnow.... see?

She bites down on her lip, slightly sinks, dipping under the water line. Sir Edward gently reaches out and lifts her back, sheet lightening floods the sky with blues and pink colors, as they kiss and sink together into the dark depths of time, watched by a million shiny twinkling stars in wonder and knowing mystical disbelief.

That night in the Waltham 1313, a stunning beautiful show of shooting coloured blue comets screamed across the silent dark black skies. All of southern England watched in knowing silence.

DAYTIME.
Strawberry pie and blueberries.

Hay grass yellow waves gently in the breeze that rolls across the top of Chingford Plain, as Kate and the new shiny strong Knight sit talking, surrounded by blueberries and big red fat strawberries. It is a conversation held while enjoying what today people would call a picnic. With a soft cream blanket and yellow pillows, the contrast between Kate, ivory pale and jet-black silver, is a contrast you could only imagine within your own private mind. It is something so very beautiful it surely could not exist in the real world itself. They talked softly, knowingly, with the odd bout of jolly laughter to break the seal of soft round words that freely flowed.

        KATE

    You see! And me only twenty-four! *(Laughter, eyes.)*

SIR EDWARD

You have the look of a sixteen ! And if I'm a day off thirty-five!

KATE

You are Sir! If a very good thirty-five be. And I am the very judge. I will take one more look, examine your

wares.

Sir Edward gives of a cheeky smile.

        KATE

No Sir, your hands, turn them upside, make them smile, er'm, I see age yes, but wisdom too, deep wisdom but some corners, you have lost (shakes her head) sorry? and now found! Which is me by the way if you had not gathered.

They gently kiss.

KATE

I taste "magic" of the pure magic kind, if I do say so myself and yes, I do so there!
It's official, you can do that again if you do wish. (smiles)

Edward

Talking of magic
your arms? (he runs he's rough hands down her pale ivory skin that sit multi colours
of swirls, circles and lines and of course magical stars) you are pure gorgeous.

Kate

Thank you, my swirls are of the old ways, ancient ways, many solid moons ago,
tribes of the "iceni" peaceful yet strong wise ancients war like beings, they had heart
of the purest kind, would fight to the very very last, women man child they knew
their worth, and these ancient blues that run free up my arms are of that and of course
stars (Kate pulls a smile then laughs)

I sound foolish like butter on meat! but it is true blue, running up and down my veins
pumping my little sweet heart with well, life!

"It is what I am!"

A gust of Skippy wind suddenly blows the yellow straw like grass "sideways"

Everything is calm......and the moon smiles round in the open daylight.

MOONS FARM.(four long miles away)

A small solid square farm house with straw thatch roof, sitting behind a round
shallow country duck pond,with green round lilies and tiny white ducks paddling
round and round, inside the little farm house of pale pinks and colored cloth stands a
women, young with straightened long cool hair so clean it shines like a polished
mirror and two multi colored ribbons fix the ends tight, her name is Alice Lorrain,
she spins with youthful excitement as her dress of many bright colours swirls round
and round.

Alice

Father!

(he looks up from stitching heavy cloth)

I will go to the great Scarborough fair ! (she stops) yet! I believe, tis true, a long and
harsh journey! (He nods)

Then I will settle for the Debden slade fair! At the Waltham, I will visit with colour
Ha ha he!
Every one will see me, I'm Alice Lorrain of moons farm!

How I will dance!!

wind sweeps across the court yard. slamming the door of the little farm shut!

Her Father just nods carries on stitching

Two normal square days pass.

GREAT AMBRESBURY HILL, dark polished night.

Stars twinkle down as a huge red fire roars into the blackness as Kate and Sir Edward laying on their backs, ponder the huge expanse of open night sky above them.

KATE

See ! great north star," pole star" constant, sits in knowing silence outside of time, watching with beaky eye!

It sees every little hidden thing.
I like that, no corners to hide, Makes me smile, turns me happy, a friend, more, family!
I talk to it, Ha! and it listens, doesn't judge, just twinkles, its seen it all, too many times, so I laugh, move on and it simply follows! Ha what a friend to have! What a friend indeed! My friend.

SIR EDWARD

Your words are smooth, yet they also" skip, jump, like beautiful energetic children, with rosy red cheeks!!

KATE

That's sweet Edward, please don't leave me? I'm not like most. I cannot move from, place to place. In real time be these true true words out in the open for all to see or laugh.

SIR EDWARD

That's a funny thing you say, I will not leave you, " I love you? "

Kate looks down, then up, smiles a short stabby smile.

KATE

Good! happiness lives with love, they are great bed fellows you know!! You, me and the Great Ambresbury, so it seems we will be here for ever and ever, it is us, family, friend, sister brother we are one, we are nature? "it is written" on stone. Painted in colour, whispered in time, Lawrence knows?

Kate pulls a funny face, as they laugh away the warm round time that sits ticking around them.

Later, same place Kate's alone.
Amsbresbury Hill dead of night looking star wards Kate lies on her back, she talks soft and gently to her self, Edwards space is empty only he's sword "English" lays next to her.

Kate is thinking...

I'm living upside down, inside out.

Worry keeps me focused, it's so near it does all my talking, so I have to break free, escape it's eye, so I look up, not to pole star but further out, and so I count upside down, inside out, as it doesn't matter there? as there is no upside down ? inside out it's all the Samish! so still I start at one, as you would? And I cross the universe like done!!!!!!!!!! and before you know it!

Worries gone, left with fear, then sweet hope turns up and holds my hand! In person warm and welcoming and so I'm now at a thousand, time does fly and I'm back, concentration brings me down with a solid grinding bump, a short nagging worry pulls at my skirt and it bites down on my nice nails, mistrust, and fear sits smiling, like big fat cats waiting for there cream, and I am that cream? so I go back to the stars where I belong, And fall into heavens deep deep sleep,

For many warm weeks the pair were inseparable; walking, laughing, Kate would sometimes be seen holding tight to the Templar's waist as they raced up the great Ambresbury hill on the huge black pumping stallion. Laughter was full and heavy in the tiny valley below and people of the Loughton talked of the great wedding at Alderton Hall. Yet Kate never left her part of the forest as each day Sir Edward would roll on down the great hill with white lily flowers or small sweet fruits.

Then, just as in every good harvest year, the travellers came, pitching their tents in the Debden Slade that sits on the verge of the forest. They came with colour and laughter and music flowed through the trees as the maypole entered the solid ground. To Kate this was a little much as she took back to her part of the forest in the cellar below Ambresbury hill.

Then from simply blue nowhere, as things usually do come, a young colourful woman, hands buried deep inside her pockets, steps out of the blue. Bells ring from the church some half a mile away the girl, " women" walks with confidence and knowing sway and on seeing Kate she smiles, then approaches, stopping only fifty feet away. She spins once just like Kate, nothing is said, it's all eyes. Thunder slightly rumbles as Kate looks to the very sky; it stops dead. The woman, is ALICE

LORRAIN, she smirks as she slowly circles her, and again she spins her cloak and words finally come forward.

ALICE

Tis true, you be Ave Kate Cellar ?   (Kate nods)

you are very thin of bone, pale of snow?
well I am Alice, Alice Lorrain of moons farm be, I'm looking for the vanity fair
on the Debden, I too am thin, see! yet big in other more important places!

Scarborough all soooo last year don't you think?
It's true what folk say….you have a way?

Futuristic…majestic maybe I to have ways" womanly" ways (stops)
You have the eyes of a Norma Jean, vintage deep solemn!
Do you drink broken bottles (smiles a crazy face)

(Then blows her a cheeky kiss, turns and starts to walk away,)

DOOO YOU ! (she shouts over her shoulder) all the beauties die you know!

Kate answer with a small tiny sniff at her with her nose then watches with mild curiosity as Alice walks a way into the distant music of the maypole dance. As a warm roll of creamy energy blows across the valley, leaves and dust fill the air as the thunder murmurs, Alice turns from the distance, she glimpses the blow and she disappears into the small maypole crowd."vanity lives"

Two long musical days pass and the red and white mayday pole is taken down. All travellers leave and that part of the forest falls happily quiet once more, just as if nothing had ever happened there.

Night time darkness rules with a sticky dark cold glue, Kate is tucked up, knees held tight to her tiny chest as stars of the diamonte kind sparkle down to her.

(she is high up in a large solid oak dreaming her dreams)

KATE *(dreams in her mind)*

I am living if that's what this is, deep deep down at the bottom of something murky' there are no straight lines just curves and it is not cold ,warm or indifferent' If I look up through the round narrowing circle, I can see a warm glowing white light. Not much, but enough for hope to survive, now people with pink rose face look on down, it is a well! I am in a well, at the very very bottom and the well is at the very top of the Great Great Ambresbury! They all come, all take, as this is a well and the water is for taking as it tastes all so very clean and sweet. So clean that small colourful fish swim on over my head as I look up, then the same fish I've seen before come back. They simply swim round and around, some even swim upside down, then something happens up there in the light - a smile, a beam it comes down with warm energy, hello, hello, hello energy, you can feel its presents tingle your skin as it passes, is there anybody there? I smile, close my eyes and disappear into the nothingness I am,

Their Fucking gone!

Kate's eyes slowly open, light smashes in as her eyelashes spring like great beautiful flowers as she wakes from her dream. greens reds blues all assault her as she stands high above the green forest floor on the hill and beams out a smile that runs tiptoe across the tree tops and into the next valley.

KATE

Hello! hello hello is there any body there? *(She smiles and childishly giggles as tiny leaves twinkle and turn around her small white English frame)*

MAY 15TH 1313 (black heavy, low clouds gather)

Morning breaks with a hollowing nasty sharp hail from the hill as Hangboy leans back, smoke, grey-green and some brown rolls peacefully across the top of the Loughton cottages that run to the edge of the forest verge. Bells softly ring out of the local church, people make their ways to service but the knight strangely doesn't come for Kate. No flowers of lilies are held, no strawberry fruit to eat, just simply plain nothing, not even a word springs to life. Snow starts to gently fall, first just little flakes then more steady. This is late May, Summer poles been and gone, yet it snows. Owls screech, crows mass in huge numbers over the boarded manor house of the Alderton Hall and people do not venture to feed their stock, yet Kate doesn't notice anything but the disappearance of her knight as she walks alone through Debden Slade over the brook. She's wearing something white like a sheep's fleece that covers the cloak she wore earlier. She sniffs the small cold breeze that runs youthfully through the valley, stopping only momentarily, then she smiles and carries on to the village. As she walks everything seemingly starts to darken, more heavy snow does fall, yet everything is not clear black and white, She stops again and turns sharply as she catches from the side of her very eye a tall cloaked monk. He walks at a distance, his head is covered by a musty, brown cotton weave. She can smell from where she stands, she knows something is very very wrong as this is no man, he's simply too tall, too solid and too dark sticky bad.

This is cold, clean Death himself and he visits her, yet he doesn't collect, just simply watches from afar, Death then gets up courage and spouts some strange square old stinking words, Kate explodes at his presence, with violence and kindred old words

.69.

that bend and snap back, Death turns and runs followed by two huge owls and a couple of smaller crows, all fighting and diving in turn on the creature that flees into the dark forest, Kate moves forwards into the tiny single road village of Loughton.

It is here that locals would often venture out and touch the bottom of her long black, twinkling dress for good luck but today no-one ventures anywhere, eventually the inn keeper closes his always-open door and all the smoke that's left in the chimneys rushes out against her friend the wind and simply runs away.

Slowly she walks on through the centre, stops and spins around quickly, Windows slam shut with a hollow bang that echoes and a small child cries with her nose to a small glass pane, slowly she makes her way back in deadly snowy white silence as she glimpses the circling huge crows above the ALDERTON HALLS roof. Then she's back to the Debden Slade and trees that cover her from the snow as she stops at the tiny bridge where Sir Edward and her first met, she gasps, falling to her knees and screams something so loud, so dark and vile, that the stream backs itself up and the water rushes in the other direction, huge white owls that watch her every move drop instantly dead and fall to the ground, Kate withers like a worm in the snowy sun holding her stomach in the deadly cold, Hang boy wails deep and dark, from the hill.

KATE

Noo noooo? Please

Then from nowhere two monks, one big the other small appear, dressed in woven hoods of chocolate colour, they pick her up and take her to her shelter. she tries to thank them, yet they have already scarpered away, hangboy wails away the hideously cold night until morning breaks with warm round sunshine, as it breaks its way through to Kate's face she blinks, smiles awkwardly and sits up, yet still from the hideous cold night ice hang down in strange shapes and crunchy frost snaps under foot, as she breaths warm air swirls out of her lips into the light

KATE

tis written. (looks down rubes her swollen stomach) is child.

For three and a half sharp days the knight did not show. Snow falls lightly, flowers of red pinks bloom out into the pure whiteness, people from the local village stay warm, keep in as grey white smoke rolls across roofs of the Loughton village that sits in the next valley.

Everything is absorbed, time moves with dragging skirt leaving the pattern on the grown.

Kate's bridge.

Snow of the bluish white kind drifts gently down, this snow is not ordinary it's heaven sent white blanket snow, it's deep, it has colour only the knowing ancient Loughton brook makes any sound that escapes it, as it maranders with trickle over the solid stones and cream smooth gravel, Kate stand alone on the bridge, her head is down like before, only momentarily does her tiny head come up, she sniffs the air.

(A fall circle in time) but this time there is no storm of water, it's to cold for that, just snow the kind of snow that absorbs you, the kind of snow that keeps your sound, like a smooth knowing blanket that covers all the sharp edges of life. and it is everywhere, simply everywhere.
Kate's toes peek out from her bleached rough dress that no longer shines with shimmer no loner has form, they are kept warm by small candles that flicker abound the bridge, everything is deadly silent....Edward appears.

face to near face, ten feet apart they stand at opposite ends of the tiny bridge.

Edward

Hello Kate.

She gasps deep with her tiny ribs, then slowly
Her small tiny head rises on these simplistic words, Edwards eyes widen like saucepans at what welcomes him.
words in black jump off the ivory white skin they say, dog betrayal, liar Kate is crazy sheik of the volatile kind, tear roll and madness lives like a king!

Edward

o my god.

This is too much for Kate to remain silent her head tilts and more tears slowly escape rolling down her cheeks, then strangely she chucks out a awkward smile to him but nothing connects as it's washed away in the stream, then courage turns up and words are born across the tiny bridge that link the pair, the words are balanced as they tip toe over the delicate silence and arrive at the night.

Kate

you forgot me…….. after everything you said.

Edward thinks as he studies her face then answer in a brash way that speak louder then he's own words.

I've been ,,,,,,,

Kate

I…..I see, s sorry for that? I just thought?

Edwards head drops down as he eyes the bridge that holds them together.

Edward

It is I who's sorry!

Kate

Is this what you do? (no answer comes back)
Was it me.
did I not smile right or or did I not bend to your liking

(Edward shakes his head)

Kate

Last time we talked u..u you lived here, inside my heart, you were my
magic
My Colour, you made me warm with your words, they swam happy sending
Me dizzy.

I could see them! taste them, You held my hand!

I breathed you in! now

You breath me out!

Kate starts to murmur, madness holds her hand as those beautiful eyes fill
With tears and she jerks towards him taking one last look into his face.

Kate

So what do I do now?

She looks intensely at him as her small tiny head slowly tilts sideways.

Kate

You have no words, your deceit is everywhere! you can smell it in the air!

You should of killed me with the sword! It would have been honest, English quick!

Edward

I'm sorry, forgive me please!

Kate

I want to….but I never get what I truly want I'm not well I can not see my Mind is squeed, everything is bad, leave me be, you are a dragon of the English kind! I see your camouflage Edward ? It hides behind your smile.

Edward

No, no!
This has not finished! Kate

Kate

For me it…is, the truth is hidden within the lie.

You said forever!! (her eyes expand like their going to burst)

Then her energy go's and her small head drops down to her chin
As she slowly backs off the tiny bridge, madness takes control, Edward watches as thousands of golden leaves full around her, they twist with the snow Kate's gone Edward stands in he's own shadow of betrayal he screams KATE! It echoes and he too leave the wooden bridge of destiny…………

Kate disappears into Debden Slade. Everything is truly deadly snowy silent, as calm settles in for a quiet night. Shooting stars bend across the black night sky and all is dead cold in the ancient hamlet of the Waltham, the year is 1313 two feet of snow lines the paths trees bend in the weight, some snap under pressure.

For nine lost hollow bleak days Kate walks in isolation through the dense forest and streams, Madness comes and goes, fear takes up position by her side as her bleached-bottomed dress sweeps the foot worn paths of the great Ambresbury. Words, bitter not sweet, are written upside down on her face with bent, sideways stars and strange patterns that jerk and twist up her thin pale neck.

She is simply lost and broken. But not completely forgotten as three massive, black, spiky crows with red beaky eyes take flight over her, they screech out like crying white ghost that can't find their ways home so they circle high above in the bluely white skies as she wonders like a fallen blurred star through her beloved yet cold forest.

(Loughton brook ankle deep she walks soaked to the brittle cold skin)

Kate (in her own sweet head)

I balance on the edge, balancing my worth,
I can see all the way down, it's very very dark
And sticky black.

I also can see up at, something I'm not quite sure of?
I think it's life, with its warm edges? Ween would now?
But I may be wrong, as wrong is seemingly what I do best?

So I balance arms out straight and I stay in bended line, see I now my place?
Now I can smell memories, sweet flowing from left to right slowly across my ivory cheek, EDWARD!! so I wobble for a second and simply hold on and try to think of times when memories where good, and then as quickly as they came they go, and I can no longer smell anything at all,
that's not pleasant, not nice at all, I take a gulp,,,, Is that some one calling in the dark maybe they need help more then me and I should go to them but I don't know where I am? Maybe it's the nothingness around me playing tricks, so now I'm wondering how long I've been here or am going to be here as it's hard to tell, that's just like life and and so I must be back! I simply must be! As I'm Kate and I see the light only small but yes up there tinkering down! And I can smell the grass!

.78.

HELLO HELLO hello, it's just me little Kate anybody there!!!
But nothing comes back, everything is hollow biscuit, everything is bad her isolation
is inside out and it echoes.

(Kate finally opens her eyes and steps out of the watery stream madness runs off
crows screech out, some seemingly laugh)

A couple of blurry days pass, night falls as the silvery stars watch in knowing
silence.

BLACK WEIRS POND BEHIND AMBRESBURY HILL.

A different colour as the brave strong knight stands looking out into the pitch
blackness. Stars watch from above as Alice Lorrain steps out of the black mass and
simply wraps her arms around the knight's strong neck, she wears a hugh white
diamond on her finger.
And she smiles, a pure "winners smile"

SIR EDWARD

your beauty is blinding Alice? your eyes light up the skies.

Alice

Thank you Edward, Stay with me, never ever leave?

SIR EDWARD

I will never leave, believe me, we are one, forever and
Ever! Under stars be I am a honorably man Alice.

They gently kiss, something they have clearly done before in time. Yet stars are not the only thing that watches in deadly cold silence, as far up in a heavy old oak, knees tucked, eyes fixed, is Kate, watching, listening, Edward lifts Alice to the huge stallion that clearly isn't happy, and Alice cuddles to the knight's back as they ride off into the blackness before them.

Kate's big swollen heart pounds deep within her tiny ribbed chest, every time she breaths out pain shoots down her tiny body, her head trembles, both her eyes are fixed solid like death at the betrayal she has just witnessed before them.

THE CURSE OF KATE'S CELLAR;

     KATE (whispers)
     O..... o
     Time has stopped, I want off.
     is this real, should I pinch my skin, bite my nails, erm LOVE
     WILL RIDE THE BACK OF SEX, till it bellows in the mud ?

She cradles herself between the huge oak branches that drift out over Black Weirs pond. Madness keeps her comfortable with giggles, she rocks, as her face jerks and frowns, tears fall slowly down into the water, catching the moon's light and fizzing out, as they hit the dark surface of Black Weirs pond, ripples run across the surface till all is once more smooth.

     Kate

Ha r, r ,? (pinches her ivory thin arm) o?
Who lingers so so late it is hard to see. In shadow and shade a maiden be, traitor he, hush, hush little darling see, as Lord's Knight Templar, he, traitor, on little me.

So vengeance be as surely as death comes to me. 'Tis demonology walking free and death he does smile, point laugh at we ... me! Therefore I here at these very hexes sport! Curse you Sir Edward knight be ... jinx on your head. As I am me, in this night just me to see I curse you, I curse you, I curse you blessed three! For all in your heaven no preacher ye!!!!

"o" "oo" "ooo"

lightning snaps in the black sky that rumbles over her and her beloved forest, and she whispers under her broken voice and tears.
Huge golden green pike with gleaming white teeth charge with force at the surface of the pond each trying to catch the tears falling from above.

Kate's words vibrate around the forest as a southwesterly wind hears her call and comes running with great mass and energy as it slams into the great Waltham.

For days the black rancid storm rolled around the massive dense forest fighting as it went, turning ancient old solid oaks into nothing but sticks and firewood, Loughton brook filled and filled turned and turned as it turned into a great winding serpent that smashed through the tiny village of Loughton, (today it's dammed by twenty foot dam)

Then, at dawn on June 15th 1313, it finally broke. Sunlight pierced the forest roof as mist rose in the heat and there before your eyes was Kate. Not the same person as before, she had been "broken" in too many places, her eyes lacked the energy and sheer beauty she held before. There in the valley itself lay her wolf, Hang boy, with sticky fur and rolled white eyes, laid out like meat for all to see, and they did as chopping bits was said to bring luck and this is what locals needed. Yet Kate did not seem to register as something in the storm had bitten her quick; opened her like a Cornish pilchard. Her power, her inner belief was battered, and taken by others yet to know their fate in history, as madness moved on in and took control. From this very moment in pure time something had changed and as many now say your lights have gone out, nobody upstairs, there are a thousand ways to describe the parcel of time that suddenly wraps itself around her or any such person or event. As when something goes wrong it doesn't just go wrong, it falls off the flipping planet!

UNDER KATE'S BRIDGE ;

Wrapped up in a bundle (dreaming)

I am walking through life
Walking through the valley of broken death

I drink broken bottles of pure glass sharpness, that slice and cut as they swallow down, I bleed inside out, nobody sees, I bleed alone inside my empty box of life, yet I still function with a girlie smile,

The world thinks I'm perfect but no, it's simple camouflage of the hidden kind and this camouflage gives me space space to go on, push forwards.

There's nothing else to do, as my time is ticking, the sticky waits, he licks his lips, he knows… I'm over before I'm really started ?

How fair's that! Who makes the rules!
So I stand to the left of line,, awkward but pretty that's the main thing the end game be pretty and smile! But I'm aching it's my tiny blue veins that run like roots up and down my ivory arms, they no longer do the pump youth, so they ache, inside blood out they are clogged thick with remorse and me just young as fun? So I look up, there heaven watches, she holding her breath? Something bigs up o my Ivory is turning grey? from the little toe up?

Sticky starts to grin his bestish with death they run as a pair a terrible terrible pair and both have breath that kills you quick!…. I turn my head, look away, leave that to another day but they keep looking on through me they are coming!

Cause I'm now seeing white angels they glide slowly down, land with gentle biscuit, no noise they make they are perfect they make pink smile out of black cabbage! And and time stops dead…. Everything is over everything is out, death stands beside me, (whispers) I can smell him…. He's all cotton muster, a kind of damp dusty keeping thing that stay longer in your nose then you want so I look down pretend he's not here then I have a terrible thought as I look down at my once white toes that are now black

The smell is me!!!! I'm living putrid I'm dying alive! From my toes up! Nobody ever said anything about that, you are either dead or alive, not still alive and being well dead! So now I feel cheated
As nothing is simple anymore!!!

O

I see silence again, he has his hands in his pockets and he sways ?
Cheated and confused everything is closing everything is over.
I want to scream out loud in real voice but someone has had me stolen and nothing comes I'm scared so so
I pull up my white cottons soaks and I do one and and I run for the sun, the warmth of life the….. stunning light hat suddenly pulls in away from the dark?

O o me?
It's sooo beautiful so clean, it's calling me in the darkness it's a beacon of life a path way to heaven! And she's flipping stunning calling me with round smooth smile quick quick! She jesters this way hurry hurry!! And I do, no second calling for me I'm off as I don't want to smell of rotten brown swede I want to smell of beautiful lilies then I jump up as something from beneath comes smashing up with sharp teeth that have my name engraved on them, so I think there for me! Right! But what every it was it missed Yet I still don't panic (I'm saving it for something special) then from the corner of me eye I see the Angels again they carry clarity that cuts through this darkness and I see the path the battle I feel is nearly over I'm nearly there but the path is narrowing just like my veins?

I feel alone, I feel like I'm the loneliest of the….what, what's that I (cough) feel in my mouth, throat lungs, I'm being filled up with the dark sticky it is staring to set in my lung, my chest feels heavy Death suddenly smiles at close call! He's trying to close me down, kick me out!

OOO, I ache like hell (and I do hope this is not a omen?) so I keep on moving, always watching out for snappers I dare not look back or down just keep pushing on Then I stop, everything is deadly silent,

I think I'm dead, think I'm over, the ache as gone? My voice cannot scream?
Memories
Float across my mind they are sweet smelling, they roll with gentle ease…..

I smile inside like a fucking child
I'm home, clarity dances, I can see! Floating as I do above the stranger that was once me just lying there all dead and that I say helloo I'm back full circle and all that, then before me I see a Angel she's of the Irish green eyed kind and she smiles?

It's ween,, Halloween we hug dance I'm fucking dead ween I scream!

Then I wake up……..and it's all a dream?
A dream fuck it, I was there I could taste it live it see it! Wasn't it real? Life then floods in and I'm awake, my head drops I must move on I must try harder. I must!

Later.

Cold veg madness.

Kate with her
Eyes down, her head low approaches a veg stall lined with plenty for all to see and buy, children stand like adults and watch her every solemn move with sniggers and wicked glee.

      STALLHOLDER to children.

Nothing for you here off with you!!!

Kate nervously looks up from the heavy voice that has just jumped her to the very core, tenderly she pulls back the cotton hood off her face exposing her red on ivory cheeks to the cold air that jumps straight on board.

KATE

Hello

Sorry, I'm very very dreadfully sorry? But can I have please yes two apples green
And some of that sweet lovely mutton how fine it looks…. Thank you sir it's a cold
day.

STALLHOLDER smiles back

Yes cold there you go, no money, just be careful take the top road yes! Your looking
tired Kate are you alright?

Kate

I'm fine thank you, your words are warm welcome please take the money sir (smiles)

STALLHOLDER

No not from you be careful? GET OFF WITH YOU!!! he again screams to the
children they scatter Kate lifts her hood turns walks down the centre of the
Loughton village as she passes some other children they taught her with a
rhyme

CHILDREN

Kate of the hollow, Kate of the pole, Kate of the hollow with a great big pole!
The witch is a bitch, the witch is a bitch, ha haaaa! look at it !!

Some apples are thrown but she doesn't stop till she sees her tiny bridge
Night falls like a warm welcome blanket on cold soiled bones over the great
Ambresbury.

The following morning mist rises like a living being. It twists and twirls in the morning light-coloured breeze that skips through the grass and up the great hill. Two locals women making their early-morning way up Pole Lane or, as today, Earl's Path, they approach the tiny little bridge over Loughton Brook "Kate's bridge"and both together stop in motion as one. Call it what you like, women's intuition or whatever, but both stop dead and turn their heads upstream where both sets of eyes find Kate.

She sits ankle deep on her bottom in the middle of the stream as the cold water rolls silently over her legs.it is a sight of strange beauty but also terrible madness as himself. Madness sits with her grinning like a cat with a small weak timed bird, and far off in the tree-lined distance you can just glimpse Death as he retreats into the deep forest, black crows swoop at him as he go's.

      Kate

I'm miles from my own mind?
Lost in tandems hope,
Drowned in morrows child,,,,, I hope heavens open?

   (Kate's eyes close as she drifts into a dream whist sitting in the brook.)

      Kate

I think,
I think I saw an angel, whilst sitting on the ocean floor *(Loughton Brook)*. My eyes open all so very slowly as something bright walks its way in telling me "Hello, it's me, you should listen to this". Watch, and as I focus, as I breath, an angel appears out of the glum. She's sweet, whitish-pink with cream coloured edges. Her dress is free-flowing with rolling movements yet she just sits in silence watching me, taking me in, wrapping me up in a warm clean parcel without any frayed edges so I will move on, speak open my little mouth and let the words flow free. And I ask her her name as politely as English mustard.

KATE

"Hello!" (A smile returns with the post.)

hope you do not mind me asking, but who are you? Sorry for being French about it."

ANGEL

I am hope, love and happiness all rolled up in one big strawberry bundle. I live just erm? there, that's it! inside at the back (points to her head)

KATE

Well, is confusious there! As panic, f fear, and family are all about!
Pointing! Laughing!

Tears silently roll down Kate's cheeks and she gulps them back.

ANGEL

Don't cry angel, ho, that's me silly thing. You are the beguiler of men, the mystical shadow that people catch from the very corner of their open eye.A futuristic star queen!... Anyone can see that! it's simple in time.

you

You are

A cuddle that makes you smile
A hug that sends you drunk
A word that keeps you…. safe and also you are the very thing you search for? don't give up, never ever give up girl?

Kate blinks and sniffles up.

ANGEL

You must leave this place Kate. You must leave now! Right now! move on into the open warm light. Move on and move up.

The angel smiles as Kate's eyes open and fall. The two women pull her out of the cold stream. Kate turns, smiles and thanks them.

KATE

ha it's j… just life squeezing me, It's difficult, lots of square edges that knock
And bruise you on the way through see, I'll be fine now, I'll be just so very,
very fine, look I'm back all puffy and clean? *(she nods herself away into the forest)*.

LOST POND, BACK OF GREAT AMBRESBURY

Next day madness sinks below the lily lined surface of the green murky pond, bubbles rise out of the mud in to the light, Kate sits alone as her space is broken; twigs snap clean and brake under careful foot, something moves in. It's Alice Lorrain dressed in every colour under the sun; red, greens, gold; fine she does look as she approaches her in this secret of all places, the lost pond (behind Ambresbury hill)

ALICE

'Tis I, Alice.

Alice looks on down at the bubbles coming up from the pond then to the broken bundle that is Kate. her eyes slowly rise up and she sniffs at the forest air, hundreds of lined black crows watch on down from the trees above.

    Kate

smells like, yes it's you.

    ALICE

I've
not come to fight.
I have news, you need to have, It is only right, fair, from women to women.

    KATE

fair, 'tis where you lies on your back, legs dangling, like worms from blackbirds beak?

    ALICE

That's not nice,,, I'm here to say my piece , ? ? I'm with…
child! A mother to be.

    KATE

I see.

Kate stands. Alice momentarily moves one step back as she nervously watches every movement around her.

ALICE

Then you see I am with child, as I've said.

KATE

yes He is that.

(Kate just looks on in deadly silence.)
ALICE

Right, Good! we will ...m, marry. At the great Hall, we will have the very very best of everything, it is our right! Yes! colours of green gold's colours of blue white we will have it all!

KATE

Of course, everything I will see to that? For history be? In perfect halo.

ALICE

Good! (shakes her head) Then that be it, I am done.

Alice goes to leave and as she spins her dress it touches the bottom of Kate's leg; every crow immediately and I do mean immediately stops crowing.

KATE

Done," yes you was, I will send white lilies with a card, Something about your name. A ... lice?

As Kate speaks these very words all the crows start chirping as if to laugh. Owls boom out as the confident Alice retreats at pace back to the wooden Alderton Hall. Kate turns herself as madness once more rises up out of the old LOST pond he is covered in green slimy lilies and takes her small pale hand. Kate falls back into a gibber as her head goes down and she fidgets with simply nothing between her small fingers as she walks. Turning, she moves through the great Ambresbury then she stops, looking down the path that towers over the green forest which sits below. There, she opens her cloak to revile her small round swollen tummy and simply runs her small pale hand around three times while small, golden leaves do fall slowly but knowingly around her. Some even glide smoothly over the hillside and out into the valley below. This brings a small but beautiful warm smile. Madness runs off as fast as he can down the steep path followed by the faithful black crows violently smashing at its head, then a warm breeze sways in over Kate and the great Ambresbury bringing with it the sweet sound of warm music from the local stone church, St Nicks, which stands on the next hill some distance away. The music fills her head, slowly sending her nearly drunk as she looks out over the great ancient Waltham forest, sweetly she murmurs then stops words are born free and they roam.

Kate

Tis written in stars, shiny see, Destiny you danced with history, fear and pain cheered
you on.
now I'm left in time too sink or swim? Ha

I can not swim, polestar what medieval magic is this and why does it hurt so
Very very much?

(thunder)

She smiles as she disappears into the dense green verge as the distant music sways in to the valley and Kate reverts back into her place of safety and awkward being, : her own fragile glass mind has crazy cracks that run and run.

(deep inside the forest)
Memories in dark closed time.

I have a memory. It's mine, ours, but I think I'm the only one who uses it, I've half share, and that keeps me safe, secure and it's wrapped up in silky fine ribbon,

Stored in bended line, darkness smiles like the creep he is.

Then one day, a day when I need it, a day I can feel it tugging, a dark cold nasty day that needs warming I put them lights on, and try and wake that sleeping memory and That beauty halo, so I, Kate, enter.

Everything is warm silent,
Everything is calm clean, the air is vacuum thin pumped, so thin it might snap as you move through, but it doesn't, its held together with corners, corners that hold.
Corners that suck up all your fucking air. So your have to forgive me but
it's a little hard to…well breath, .. And that's important so

I try, and I'm in

So I look left, slowly then right,
Dust floats silently, like golden church heaven, light flickers, and just there, a line of, of square shaped boxes, all in line (well they would be?) and they have square shaped edges and sharp pointed ends that could cut and bruise you on the way through!

So I'm careful, I keep my elbows tucked. (like a duck in the pan)

Then as I look along I see surrounded, hemmed. A round colorful sweet small box, it has different ribbon to the others, and in a funny way it sits on its own? yet still surrounded?

They want her air, they might attack! violence might lurk

But she takes no notice, carries on collecting dust, she's happy that way, yet
She is not weak, not white silk, as she is covered in a hard shiny shell, it's mint and
tough you would not dare to stare her in the eye, but inside that toughen shell well
she's you know? and so I breath out with a beautiful shy that leaves me a little drunk,
dizzy, but then again I've not eaten for days and being drunk might be a state of
mind, so a little light headed but standing I reach up, lift it down, it seems
undamaged, light heavenly, only a couple of tiny blurred finger prints to show any
ones been here, and they are mind, all mine? So I smile as you do when meeting a old
friend, and yes it's the very same smile that existed back then on that very day I
boxed up. A memory lived, and so I say Hello hello hello, as politeness is an English
virtue, and I'm back!! Sweetness lives.

I can smell it, taste it, own it, it is me, my past! And as soon as I have this back,
everything starts to go dim, and them big boxes start to close, the smell disappears,
stolen, I'm on my own, black darkness grins. like he's says (told you so) ??

I move on, I've no option, I'm out of date! My time has maybe come? And so I smile
upside down but it does not matter as nobody can see, NO BODY.

It's just me, Katie and nobody knows me.

I have no friends, they are all but dead.
So I sit in a great big hollow! A box ?.....well that's how it seems !!
Square, dusty, inside it's..... dark the kind of dark that can sometimes live inside your
head, but then again not to dark to see the sharp sticky corners that spy you, the
corners that go nowhere and maybe that's me. I go nowhere, maybe I don't event
exists and this is one Hugh silent funny joke.

Everyone laughs but there's no one here?

I'm a joke in a box! And no one sees, the hidden joke, Kate of the Ambresbury ha ha!

So I gulp down the dusty square air that sticks in my throat, tingles my being and I
shout out in weaken voice.

Hellooo
       hellooo
              (whispers) …..helllooooooo.

I wait my time as good things always comes to those who wait? I've said this before!
And nothing comes back. Not even my own echo wants me now.

That's not what a girl wants to hear.
What a girl wants to feel, deep down amongst the mushrooms of life, so maybe my
Echo's. The one I born has been captured?

By the echo capturer, and is kept in a rusty Iron cage with big heavy locks and
prodded once a day just to make sure it gives me up, sells me out, then again maybe
it wanted to fly, it's big chance, to run see the world, run through knee high green
grass that waves in the breeze?

If so, I wish you well echoooo! baby go do your thing!!

Now my head go's down, slowly majestically, I pull from under a small loanly smile
whilst viewing my white pebbles that stick on the ends of my white pale sticks I

Wiggle 1 2 3 ???????? Hold on? WHAT! I'm not alone, no look!!!
It's Ween!! My only friend in history!

I new it was you, I'd recognize them whites anywhere's girl!
Long time no see!
But Ween never spoke; never used words of simplistic form she simply talked with
her eyes, me and her our own hidden language it was special! Mystical.

So we sat in a parcel of rosy pink time. Ween and I.

and

We dangled in white tandem ankle. surrounded by shiny shiny stars

It was pure vintage of the finest kind as we sipped back golden cool copper
Cider.

Well that's how it seemed to me, how it felt, how it ran,

Under skin, under brittle clean biscuit.

So Ween and I dangle.
Over?? Over my bridge as water bubbles through, rushing along just like the copper
cider, hurrying to do it's thing, it's job to make me

Smile.
Grin.
Laugh and be silly.

Me and Ween.

Ween of fragile beauty, delicate silk.
She wore Emerald eyes. So very very green when you looked in you never came out,
as they kept growing, welcoming, hugging.

My friend Ween

Her dress skips with tender white hip.
Her medieval flow is golden silence and her tender tip of toe is holly brought!!

   Then we come to her cream da la cream.
   Her lime blue pink yellow.

Sensitivity with a little baby,   s. (said all so quietly)

Which she carried on her tender white hip.
Mystical marvel of a medieval way her beauty sways she is simply mint delicate.

So I breath easy, softly don't won't to upset, knock bruise.

She's my friend
My reclusive natured friend; Ween.

Sent down from heaven.
White angles flock to see her Emerald glow, her beam, her beacon of sensitivity that
flashed out into the cold desolate world!

A world of brittle biscuit.

A world with sharp edge that slices in deadly silence!

But my slice was Ween, A pure cream fancy with white cream topping mouth
watering.

Everyone wants.

Ween the Moorish!!!

I too hold up my hands, I wanted to cherish hold mother?

Stay away she's....delicate.
A beauty of white lily on green golden pond.
When we'd meet I'd say in a girly way

Hellooooo Ween!! ha

Her tiny head would go down and bubbles of golden copper giggles would rise up
and escape from the round edges, then she'd pop up again with a tender smile just for
me, but no words never words, they where course, common and she did not need
them it was all the old ways with us.

A look.
A glance.

We just new a belief of the natural kind she could turn heads from behind!

Magic pure magic

No words said in open : the reclusive Ween of sensitivity.
We dangled under the stars under pole star over my bridge, I'd spill in gentle tone,
softly verbs nothing to harsh and she just tilted her Irish emerald head and took me
all in like a book, all eyes glowing back like a warm fire that keeps you warm,
Mystical polite ha !

I always said with a smile

Politeness is a beautiful tool used in the right way it will open most things that are
worth opening, but strangely it did not open Ween, she was not to be opened too
deep people would fall in and you'd never see them again!

She had it all so plain blue cool on white pure lily blue.
 Then out of that very blue
   Out of the lily fucking white….the green was gone?

Suicide pie it's time to die.

Found under bridge, sleeping water, Emeralds wake cider bubbles.

She, she left vellum. A note in time to…me.. bloody ME!

To my
AVA KATE CELLAR below the great Ambresbury

I'm sinking in the sticky.
Up to my very chin.
It's dark, cold, I'm scared hollow.

I wished I had talked. Opened spilled, wish that I wasn't so so delicate, now I'm broke the sticky is within.
Setting itself at home.

It's cold girl. no longer can I feel my hands, my white sticks.
I am sinking Kate going down, down the silence has me by the waist, it has firm grip, so I need to speak fast and these are my words, that I roll to you.

My
Tears are cast in heaven
Heaven is where I sleep
Sleep is with that person
I really had to meet in silver stars be

That's you !   AVE KATE CELLAR

I love you

Did at the very moment we meet, no more words could be spoken everything was suddenly so so clear it was you that lived in my heart you that I carry with me in to the sticky so I'm not alone, sorry for leaving, please don't cry I promise we will live again in the black and white !!

I will wait a 1000 blue moons take ca....

....time passes.........

Nobody knows where's weens body is buried, some say she was left in the pool going round and round, locals to scared to pull her out just in case something pulled them in. One thing we do know is she fell for Kate Cellar and in her sensitivity she kept it to herself and I'm sure Kate would never of left her going round and round, that's if Ween ever existed in the real world as it seems, just maybe, Ween was in fact Kate her self playing her own beautiful dreams within a dream? Nobody will ever know. She was only mention on a few occasions, always reclusive, always shy, always Ween.

Months pass as one becomes two. A little baby gorgeous girl is born to life (no name have we) and carried beneath the heavy cottoned cloak of stars and moons that protect her, snow, rain, frost all came in battalions, yet every fall round bluish moon, Kate would be seen sitting on the tiny arched bridge that broke the Loughton brook beneath it, deep within the forest.

It would be covered from head to toe with flowers of lilies and candles, There they would wait, Kate sitting and jangling her tiny legs over the side of the little bridge that spans the stream that runs all the way through Kate's forest. From early evening she would be there waiting for her knight to show, people would leave gift's of food and drink as they passed hurrying away to there warm beds in the Loughton village, Sometimes she would go right through and out the other side, no words were heard or, come to that, no crying either from the baby. they simply just held their own ground in their own solid way, Then one warm still evening Kate looks up and then around as the very night starts to wake. No birds sing, no owls talk; it is deadly still as everything turns dark and the night settles in. Kate sits as always with legs swinging over the edge watching the newborn sleep in its basket of weave and soft cream cloth. It is a very dark night, the kind of dark seen just before death. Yet she is surrounded by her warm glowing candles that flicker and somewhat keep away the deadly cold. Then before what seems a mere hour the very morn starts to break. Kate jumps up, looks south then north up the great hill, tears beginning to swell at the nothingness before her. Just before the morn fully awakes Kate speaks out with true passion and warm English heart.

KATE

Knight, if you hear this, then show yourself to me, as not for little me, but
daughter be!

She spins twice, thunder roars low and far in the distance. Everything starts to go
dim as the very blue moon in the morn sky stands up to the warm morning sun that
has just beamed, and moves slowly across its very face, darkness lives and the night
comes back, slowly at first then to "total eclipse." Kate's eyes expand like plates;
energy snaps and sparks, as strange awkward sounds vibrate around them, She stands
defiantly on her tiny bridge. Everything goes deadly black and she talks in the pure
time to her lost lost knight.

KATE

I here you, before we haunt?
I hear you; I hear you diamond solid knight, not in words but in time be, You
do not visit us or see us safe but you send this message plain to me in history
and pure white time, do not be sad for us, do not cry; as we are the night, the
day, the trees that bend and sway, do not linger at our fate as crocodile be, so
from me to you in this hidden hidden history see a "tale is written," a dragon
be? for me to fight and for you to flee and for all those people that read our tale
remember, remember, remember ME eeeee!

The warm morning sun
breaks through. snow falls bleachy white, Kate is gone; just the flowers of white and
red and burnt out candles remain on the tiny tiny bridge.

Kate's bridge today.

Kate's bridge looking up path to the great
Ambresbury Hill

One by one the tiny white candles fizzle out, then, thirteen minutes later, the sound of a heavy horse galloping at pace and speed comes down the great hill. Sir Edward stops violently as his huge black stallion spins in a nervous but predictable way, before the tiny bridge and looks down at the candles and flowers and nervously spins once more. golden leaves twinkle down around the bridge, and the night draws he's loyal friend "English" it catches the light, then Sir Edward assualts the forest with words that come up from deep within he's own heart.

SIR EDWARD screams!!

Kate!.....

Kate!.....

These are my words

Born to me

In history

Surrounded in battle a circle see!
At this we bridge a traitor me.

So I Edward, knights Templar roll my words to you Kate
please please forgive me be.

Your time in history, you will see?

A Demon me
A Dragon see

So I bite my tongue and search for thee!

In blackness,……and eternity!

We will meet again!
A circle see, on your bridge.

Just you and….me in history

Leaves fall, Edwards head drops and the horse bolts away at speed

Everything is deadly silent, event to this very very modern day if you stand on the tiny half round bridge you will see something of the silence that still remains.

The kind off silence just before a storm, a kind of silence so deep if you fell in you would never ever come back out as the same person whom went in?

GREAT STORM OF 1313, END GAME BUT ONE.

All that strange awkward rancid day everything seemed different, bent and twisted sideways, as the locals stayed put in their thatched cottages as the great marshes of the Thames flooded deep. It is not every day that morning comes twice as surely once is enough for any dear mortal. Birds snuggled their way deeper and deeper into their nests, whilst pure panic overtook the great hall of the Alderton. Sir Edward took flight with Alice, riding off at a pace of pure white fear, as Death waved them by. A warm gentle breeze took hold throughout the great forest coming from deep out in the southwesterly. All that day she grew and she grew. By night the massive oaks bent and creaked with pure knowing energy and there upon the great Ambresbury Hill, lights shone out high and strange beautiful music covered the forest floor and thousands upon thousands of crows swayed in.

A massive circle of energy above the trees and hill. Huge white snowy owls joined at a lower level. All the locals watched in pure white fear as Sir Edward and Alice, now some miles away, turned at the awesome sight they were leaving behind them. And there right in the very, very core of the Great Ambresbury dances a lone beautiful, small, ivory figure; 'tis … Kate stands with paint on skin.

Spining with pure white energy her grace painted in blues reds and gold and adorned dance with the dangerous winds that spin and start to snap at the very core of the hill. The wind digs deep gullies and troughs into the ground yet Kate, knowing, dances on as every branch, and leaf moves with her and the strange wild exploding music.

All that dark, electric snapping night thunder roared and lightening span upon the great Ambresbury Hill uprooting massive thousand-year-old trees that went back even further in time then this very story itself.

Then it was over, peace breaths like a new born child, and Kate dangles over her tiny bridge, it's morning the very calm after the storm, mists swirls as Kate watches the smoothed patterned water flow freely in circles beneath her two white sticks, then from pretty sweet know where two small perfectly round bubbles break the surface followed by a stunning ivory head it's female and it smiles at her before ejecting spouting water from it's sweet oval mouth, a connection made?

Kate

Hello Ween, what you doing?

Ween (speaks in round soft words)

I'm waiting Ave Kate cellar, for you....swimming round and round like a little lost
fish? I think I'm found? (ween slowly sink under then back up she's all eyes)
How long you going to be, I'm dying to talk.

Kate

We will talk mystical, our ideology will survive, live grow! From a tiny look, a side
ways stair or a beautiful sky or storm! This is me, this is you?

We will live in cotton paper, we will move on silver screen! We will run like children
Across peoples minds, in our own hidden silence.

See!

We live in patterns, dream in dreams.
I am wading through memories

I carry flowers in my eyes (points to ween)
Wishes in my pockets

My dress is made of hope....and there's not much of it
I wear rainbows of silver star dust
Glitter of winter smiles   I'm coming ween?

Ween flashes lash smiles and sinks below the surface Kate closes her eyes
Time stops mists roll then she take a small animalistic sniff of the air her eyes shoot
open her back straightens something is there behind her on her tiny bridge, she can

smell it feel it, it's presents is so strong she can taste the awkward tang, slowly she stands rolls up her tiny fabric that covers her arms revealing beautiful blue and gold patterns of the warrior kind, her head go's down, mist and now noise of movement come from the surrounding forest, men with flags a army of broken ghostly figures surround her bridge then she turn sharp like to cut, and there before her on her tiny bridge that sit in her forest

Stands History

He carries the heavy sword of time, Kate's head comes up she looks him face to face only ten feet apart, a soldier with a flag chucks Kate a silver sword, the others immediately kill him in the mash that he stands, Kate grails, sparks fly as she strikes at him.

They fight through the mash and in the stream watched on by histories ever moving army before they are back on the bridge, everything comes full circle, a pattern is formed, Kate is broken, exhausted she can hardly hold up the sword and history knows at the end of the day he is the only ever winner then crying is heard it comes from a basket at the very side of the bridge it's Kate's child all eyes are on the basket then Kate drops immediately to one knee in front of History every one cheers as Kate lowers her sword and bails before him.

The mist of time rises up
History like always marches slowly on.

Each soldier picks up a pebble from the stream and leaves it on the bridge.

3 short days later in the early frosty morn a local man fetching water from the pond looked on in amongst the white creamy lilies and there at the bottom of the usually peaty pond was Kate. Looking back up, surrounded by crystal clear water, History tall and strong looked on from afar as it took a day to pull her out and to drag her body out and up the bank. People say she had a beamy knowing rosy smile upon her young smooth ivory face. As they opened her cloak they found the baby, it too with a knowing warm smile, locals carried her flower born body shoulder high through the forest in a beautiful procession.

The warren pond Chingford, this is where Kate and her child lie
overlooking the lake, keeping watch, and the two small oaks placed
on their graves have now in seven-hundred years wrapped each other up as the two
oaks became one, entwined in pure time itself.

HOPE COVE, DEVON. STILL MORE STRANGE GOINGS ON.

Locals told of a strange event on that night of great storms. As they fastened their
boats in the cove, some talked about a party or music with swirling owls and
thousands of black crows circling around and around the great Bolt's Tail cliff. They
spoke of a small-framed figure dancing on top of the Greystone that juts out over the
cliff. Even to this very day the crows still wait for the return of Kate.

Then three long tired years on a grey and broken Sir Edward and Alice returned to
Alderton Hall. Nobody welcomed them and the colours had faded on the house but
they stayed. Sir Edward could be seen watching at the great hill until this got too
much and he took to his bed. Alice too withered and wrinkled into madness. One
morning the new maid took Sir Edward's son down to Black Weirs pond where she
stopped and smiled at the thousands of flowers circling the pond. She leaned down to
pick them from the forest floor. The young boy, now three, ran over to the pond's
edge and looked into the deep and somewhat dark peaty water as leaves began to fall
from the overhanging oak trees. The maid looked up to hear the little boy whispering
to himself as he peered down into the watery depths.

BOY

Look! stars Martha! Look at the stars! Is there anybody there? Hello, hello?
Is there anybody there? Hello?

With these very last words of "Hello"he reached down and laughed as a small child's
pale hand gently pulled him into the hidden depths of Black Weirs pond. Rain gently
falls, all was silent, all was dead, as the small childish laughter grew and Martha ran
back to the great Hall in pure medieval panic.

Kate's curse had been served. And as she sleeps in peace and pure white time, remember, if the leaves do fall before you in any forest you should always whisper, quietly mind, under your very shallow breath, "Kate's Cellar, Kate's Cellar, Kate's Cellar three" as all good things come in threes. This will bring you the luck Kate never never got.

The ancient carving of Kate's Cellar

"K.C."

By Lawrence .R. Hall

So the ink is dry
The book is written
The ideology of Ave Kate Cellar
Star * of Epping Forest and deep
Thinking witch lives on.

Embellished by words
Stylized by beauty
Now hopefully she has danced
Out of the sticky and in to your minds

Carry her well and remember
As she would say,
Everything is written.
It is written in the sky

.114.

Poem

Pebble with a smile

The ideology of Ave Kate Cellars mind

I am a shiny round silent white pebble
I've no edge, no beginning no end
I sit at the bottom of a deep deep dark silent pond

Nobody sees
Nobody hears (fact)

I am my own best friend
So I wait
Do my own thing
Wear my own silent thoughts

Yet I do have hope
        Do have inspirations......of the round pebble kind

It's what I am, and I roll with them
As I roll I dream
It's a personal thing that sits under lock and heavy rust key

But I will tell you this between me and you

I dream see
I dream a good dream, a crystal fucker that's got plaited hair and a great big smile
I've practice
        It's what I do
                What I'm trained for
It's ingrained inside me...I'm not hollow

My dreams roll, my dreams smile
You can carry them in your pockets and take them to heaven if you wish
Then there's the big one that explodes silver star dust
The one that's bigger then the rest
A dream that could change your life
A dream that falls from silent heaven

Answers all the questions in life with a simple, look, smile!
Dreams that could wash you out of the everyday murk of life and sweep you away
into the river of movement
                              Pace, things going on, but I don't close my eyes I'm vigilant

I pass broken bottles, broken dreams that are snagged
Yet mines not broken, not snagged
I keep rolling along

Then I stop…things settle
Murk still lives, rubbish floats (it always does)

This is not a dream, this is a nightmare before the dream!
So I try to swim, keep in the race, but well I'm a pebble, a stone and so I gently settle
again

It's what we do in life
I settle right up to my rim and this is not murk or slimy dank silt it's fine clean sand
that hugs my shape

I'm comfy

It's seen my kind before…so I sit
Look up everything is clearing
I can see heaven
It smiles warmth and

I taste salt!

I'm in the sea !

Cleaver me.....they said I was going nowhere!
Well I have now
Look at me
On the beach of Rosie life
Showing my curves
Giving out paleness without shame
Look how far I've come

Little me from dark dank vile of life
I smile, waves crash like rolling magic silver seahorses
Colour laughs, it's all going on!

I'm the fucking pebble on the beach!!

Who'd of thought !!
Who'd of dreamt   !!

I smile what a life! What a dream! What a beach !

Goodbye.

THE END